Kayden/Simon

Also From Alexandra Ivy

GUARDIANS OF ETERNITY
When Darkness Ends
Darkness Eternal
Hunt the Darkness
Embrace the Darkness
When Darkness Comes

MASTERS OF SEDUCTION
Volume One
Masters Of Seduction Two
Reckless: House Of Furia

ARES SERIES
Kill Without Mercy

BAYOU HEAT SERIES
Bayou Heat Collection One
Bayou Heat Collection Two
Angel/Hiss
Michel/Striker
Ice & Reaux

BRANDED PACK
Stolen and Forgiven
Abandoned and Unseen

DRAGONS OF ETERNITY
Burned by Darkness
Scorched by Darkness

SENTINELS
On The Hunt

Also From Laura Wright

INCUBUS TALES

SPURS, STRIPES and SNOW Series
Sinful in Spurs

Kayden/Simon

Bayou Heat Novellas

By Alexandra Ivy & Laura Wright

1001 Dark Nights

EVIL EYE
CONCEPTS

Kayden/Simon
Bayou Heat Novellas
By Alexandra Ivy & Laura Wright

1001 Dark Nights
Copyright 2016 Alexandra Ivy & Laura Wright
ISBN: 978-1-942299-29-5

Foreword: Copyright 2014 M. J. Rose
Published by Evil Eye Concepts, Incorporated

Acknowledgments From The Authors

From Alexandra:

For the men in my life. David, Chance and Alex

From Laura:

Love and thanks to the wonderful and very brilliant duo of Liz Berry and MJ Rose. So proud to be a part of this kickass world!

Sign up for the 1001 Dark Nights Newsletter
and be entered to win a Tiffany Key necklace.

There's a contest every month!

Go to www.1001DarkNights.com to subscribe!

As a bonus, all subscribers will receive a free
1001 Dark Nights story
The First Night
by Lexi Blake & M.J. Rose

One Thousand and One Dark Nights

Once upon a time, in the future...

*I was a student fascinated with stories and learning.
I studied philosophy, poetry, history, the occult, and
the art and science of love and magic. I had a vast
library at my father's home and collected thousands
of volumes of fantastic tales.*

*I learned all about ancient races and bygone
times. About myths and legends and dreams of all
people through the millennium. And the more I read
the stronger my imagination grew until I discovered
that I was able to travel into the stories... to actually
become part of them.*

*I wish I could say that I listened to my teacher
and respected my gift, as I ought to have. If I had, I
would not be telling you this tale now.
But I was foolhardy and confused, showing off
with bravery.*

*One afternoon, curious about the myth of the
Arabian Nights, I traveled back to ancient Persia to
see for myself if it was true that every day Shahryar
(Persian: شهریار, "king") married a new virgin, and then
sent yesterday's wife to be beheaded. It was written
and I had read, that by the time he met Scheherazade,
the vizier's daughter, he'd killed one thousand
women.*

Something went wrong with my efforts. I arrived in the midst of the story and somehow exchanged places with Scheherazade – a phenomena that had never occurred before and that still to this day, I cannot explain.

Now I am trapped in that ancient past. I have taken on Scheherazade's life and the only way I can protect myself and stay alive is to do what she did to protect herself and stay alive.

Every night the King calls for me and listens as I spin tales. And when the evening ends and dawn breaks, I stop at a point that leaves him breathless and yearning for more. And so the King spares my life for one more day, so that he might hear the rest of my dark tale.

As soon as I finish a story... I begin a new one... like the one that you, dear reader, have before you now.

Legend Of The Pantera

To most people the Pantera, a mystical race of puma-shifters who live in the depths of the Louisiana swamps, have become little more than a legend.

It was rumored that in the ancient past, twin sisters, born of magic, had created a sacred land and claimed it as their own. From that land was born creatures who were neither human or animal, but a mixture of the two.

They became faster and stronger than normal humans. Their senses were hyper acute. And when surrounded by the magic of the Wildlands in the bayous of Southern Louisiana, they were capable of shifting into pumas.

As the years passed, however, the sightings of the Pantera became so rare that the rumors faded to myths.

Most believed the entire species had become extinct.

Then months ago, they'd been forced to come out of the shadows when it was uncovered that a secret sect of humans have been experimenting with Pantera blood and DNA.

It's a battle for the future of the puma-shifters.

One they dare not lose.

No matter what the cost.

Kayden

Chapter One

Success.

Grim satisfaction surged through Kayden Segal as he rose to his feet with a speed that knocked his chair backward.

A handful of fellow Geeks glared in his direction before returning their attention to their computers that were stationed side by side on a long table in a cramped, dark room.

Since the official headquarters of the Pantera had been destroyed by a suicide bomber, the computer specialists had been forced to use temporary lodgings that were hastily built in the center of the Wildlands. The overcrowded space had only served to further fray the nerves of the puma shifters that had already been scraped raw by the recent attack. None of them had been prepared for the brash intrusion by Christopher Benson's soldiers. Or for the plot to destroy the computer files that the Pantera had managed to steal from Benson Enterprises.

Thankfully most of the Geeks were all too preoccupied with restoring the files from the remote servers to pay attention to Kayden as he pocketed his phone and headed out of the narrow, wooden cabin.

Although he'd been working as hard as the rest of his people to discover what Christopher Benson had been so anxious to destroy, he'd had a secondary mission.

After all, as devastated as they'd been by the various skirmishes over the past months, the Pantera had managed to inflict their own share of damage on their enemies. Which meant that their security had been compromised.

It was during his search through the files they'd managed to steal from a lab in New Orleans a few months ago that his life had been changed forever.

But it wasn't until this moment that he finally had the last piece of the puzzle.

* * * *

Xavier, the leader of the Geeks, winced at the noise assaulting his sensitive ears.

The center of the Wildlands was usually bustling with activity. It was the heart of the pack. The area where the Pantera gathered to enjoy meals and watch the cubs play in the dappled sunlight.

Over the past few weeks, however, it'd been crowded with the temporary shelters used by the various factions—Diplomats, Geeks, and Hunters—while the main headquarters was being rebuilt.

Standing at the edge of the clearing, the two males studied the roof being nailed down on the large, colonial-styled structure. The new headquarters would look a lot like the old one, although it would be larger, with the latest technology built in.

Xavier had just received an update from the electrician who was preparing to install the solar panels. He was a tall male with mocha-toned skin and brilliant blue eyes. He had powerful shoulders, a broad chest, and sharp features that were emphasized by the buzzed cut of his dark hair.

Beside him was Raphael, the head of the Diplomats. He was equally tall, although his frame was lean rather than heavily muscled, and his blond hair was long enough to brush his shoulders. His eyes were jade, until his inner puma was aroused. Then they smoldered a pure gold.

The two alphas had been working closely together to not only repair the damage from the recent attack, but to reassure their people they were doing everything in their power to keep them safe.

Xavier was just filling in Raphael on the status of the electronic surveillance they were installing on the border of the Wildlands when he caught sight of the male Pantera strolling toward him with a grim determination.

Kayden.

The younger male was a fellow Geek with short dark hair that always looked messy to Xavier, but his mate told him was mussed in a sexy way.

Just as she claimed that Kayden's neatly trimmed goatee was sexy. Whatever. Women were the strangest creatures.

The male's eyes were a dark gold that changed to cognac when he was in his cat form. His features were lean, and his skin a rich shade of bronze. At the moment he was wearing a cream knit sweater and charcoal gray pants. The early February weather was gray and chilled, with a persistent drizzle falling from the low clouds.

"Sorry to interrupt," Kayden said, not sounding a bit sorry as he came to a halt directly in front of Xavier.

Xavier arched a brow. He could practically feel the tension radiating from the younger male.

"What's going on, Kayden?"

"I need a few days off," he said, the words clipped.

"A few days for what?" Xavier demanded.

Kayden's lean face gave nothing away. "It's personal."

Xavier scowled. He knew that he could be unreasonable at times. Especially since the attack. But his nerves had been scraped raw.

"You do realize we're in the middle of war?" he snapped.

"I've been doing my part," Kayden reminded him, the air heating with his irritation even as his expression remained stoically calm. As if his inner emotions were so intense he had to keep them locked down tight. "I didn't sleep for a week after the attack."

"Yeah, I know. Shit." Xavier scrubbed his hand over his face, sharing his fear. "I can't lose any more friends, Kayden."

"You're not losing me," Kayden assured him. "I'll be back."

The words did nothing to ease Xavier's fear. "Can you at least tell me where you're going?"

A tight smile stretched Kayden's lips. "To collect on a long overdue payment."

Without waiting for Xavier's blessing, the male turned to stride away, his back stiff.

Xavier gave a frustrated shake of his head. "I was afraid of that," he muttered.

Raphael tilted his head to the side. "Trouble?"

Xavier turned to meet Raphael's curious gaze. "Kayden is one of my best. He created the program we're using to retrieve the corrupted files we stole from the Benson Enterprises computers."

They'd just recently discovered that the scientists who worked for

Christopher Benson had had been capturing Pantera and using them in their sick experiments for years.

"Surely you can spare him for a couple of days?" Raphael pointed out. "We've been working ourselves to the point of exhaustion. It might be a good idea for all of us to consider some time off to charge our batteries."

Xavier didn't have to ask if Raphael was thinking about taking a few days to enjoy his mate and new baby. It was etched on his goofy expression.

The same one that crossed Xavier's face when he thought of his own mate.

"I wouldn't mind if I truly thought he was recharging his batteries," he admitted.

"What do you think he's doing?"

"Searching for the man who was responsible for killing his parents."

Raphael stiffened, his eyes smoldering with flecks of gold, his cat prowling close to the surface.

"I thought they died when their plane crashed somewhere in Death Valley?" he growled.

"It's what we all thought after we were contacted by the FAA," Xavier conceded. "But, neither the plane nor the bodies were ever recovered."

"Christ." Heat sizzled through the air. "Are you saying they didn't die?"

Xavier's jaw clenched. For years they'd allowed themselves to become so isolated from society, they hadn't realized that there was an evil human who'd created an entire industry that centered on kidnapping them to use as laboratory rats.

Now they were trying to discover just how much damage had been inflicted while they'd been hiding in the bayous.

"Kayden recently hacked into a database that listed the captives that had been taken by our enemies over the past fifty years," he explained.

A low growl rumbled in Raphael's throat. "Bastards."

Xavier held up his hand. "Preaching to the choir, dude."

Raphael sucked in a deep breath, struggling to control his temper.

None of them were capable of discussing Christopher Benson or his henchmen without wanting to have them forced into the Wildlands where they could rip them to shreds with their fangs and claws.

"Did Kayden find something?" he at last asked.

Xavier slowly nodded his head. "A male and female were abducted outside the San Francisco Airport on the exact day his parents' private flight left and supposedly crashed in the desert."

Raphael's brows drew together. "He can't be sure it was them."

Xavier shrugged, not surprised by the words. If they'd learned nothing else over the past months, it was to never assume anything.

"That's what I told him, so he kept digging," Xavier said.

Raphael's lips twitched. "I don't doubt that Kayden managed to turn over every stone."

"He's obsessed," Xavier agreed. Kayden had always been intense. Losing his parents had wounded him deeply. Now that he suspected it was more than a senseless accident, he was consumed with the need to discover the truth. "Especially now."

"What did he find?" Raphael asked.

"Pictures."

"Pictures?" Raphael clenched his hands. "Of his mother and father?"

"Yes."

The scent of angry puma laced the chilled air as Raphael went into hunter-mode.

"They're alive?" he demanded.

Xavier grimaced. "No. The records show they were killed almost twenty years ago in one of Benson's Frankenstein laboratories."

Raphael released his breath on a frustrated hiss. "Shit."

"My thought exactly," Xavier muttered.

Raphael glanced toward the tangled foliage that carpeted the spongy ground and circled around the thick patches of cypress trees.

"So where do you think Kayden is going?" the Hunter asked, his expression worried.

Xavier was equally worried. Kayden possessed a razor-sharp intelligence, and an ability to fully focus on a problem until it was solved. He also possessed a swift temper that had been stoked to the point of combustion by the revelation his parents had been murdered by their enemy.

"He was searching for the scientist responsible for conducting the lethal experiment on his parents," Xavier said.

"You think…" Raphael's words trailed away.

"I think he found him," Xavier completed the worrisome thought.

Chapter Two

The Cruise Clinic was built deep in the Sonoran Desert.

Surrounded by sharp hills and saguaro cacti, it was a three-story building covered by an orangish adobe that blended into the landscape. It was a highly secretive laboratory where Joshua Ford and his team of scientists worked on cutting edge cancer research.

Less than a mile away was a private house that had a Spanish flavor with long wings and an inner courtyard that was decorated with a large fountain and mosaic floor. The roof was covered with red clay tiles, and the arched windows offered a perfect view of the distant mountains.

It was a beautiful home, with enough space to house a small village. But Bianca Ford found herself pacing with restless dissatisfaction from one end of the long living room to the other.

At the age of twenty-two, it wasn't unreasonable that she often felt trapped by living in the middle of nowhere. Especially since her weekly treatments to contain her cancer meant that she couldn't actually move away.

Tonight, however, her sense of claustrophobia was ten times worse than usual.

She didn't know why. The day had been perfectly normal. But over the past hour, her skin felt too tight for her body, and there was an odd knot of agitation that was lodged in the pit of her stomach.

As if there was something inside her trying to get out.

Unnerved by the sensations, Bianca had grabbed a light jacket and pulled it over her jeans and dark jade sweater. Her long, straight blonde hair was pulled into a ponytail, and her oval face, dominated by a pair of hazel eyes, was scrubbed clean of makeup.

All she wanted to do was take a long walk in the hopes of burning off the odd burst of adrenaline that was tingling through her.

Predictably, her desire was destined to be thwarted as Donald, her no-neck behemoth of a bodyguard, had refused to unlock the doors, claiming that it was too dangerous to be outside. In a rare fit of temper, she'd insisted that her guard tell her father that she wanted to speak with him.

Ten minutes later a tall, slender man with sharply carved features and thick, salt-and-pepper hair that was always perfectly groomed stepped into the room.

A pair of cold, clinical blue eyes studied her as Joshua Ford precisely arranged the cuffs of his starched shirt that was chosen to perfectly match the dove gray suit and dark blue tie.

He looked at her like she was a smudge of cells on a petri dish.

Her father had always been devoted to her welfare, Bianca silently acknowledged. But she'd never been certain if he was devoted to *her.*

Instantly she grimaced, trying to squash the disloyal thought.

"Good evening, my dear," Joshua murmured, stretching his lips into a smile. "Donald said that there was a problem?"

She hunched a shoulder, suddenly feeling like a misbehaving child. Although her father's expression was bland, she knew he was annoyed to have his immaculately planned schedule disrupted.

"Not precisely a problem," she muttered. "I simply wished to go for a walk."

A silver brow arched. "At this hour?"

She understood his confusion. It was only seven o'clock, but dark had fallen over an hour ago.

"I need some fresh air," she tried to explain.

"Fine." He gave a small shrug. "If you need to be outside, why not use the courtyard? That's why I had it built, after all."

She wrinkled her nose. "I want to walk, not go in circles."

His lips tightened. Still, he maintained a firm control over his temper.

"I really think it would be better if you wait until tomorrow."

"Why?"

"You know quite well that the desert can be a dangerous place. There could be any number of predators lurking in the dark."

It was true. That didn't, however, ease her unreasonable urge to be out, running beneath the moon.

The crazy impulse refused to leave her in peace.

"I won't go far," she said.

He gave a click of his tongue. "Please don't press this, Bianca."

She furrowed her brow. "I wish you would tell me what's going on."

The blue eyes managed to become even more frosty. Clearly she'd hit a nerve.

"I have no idea what you mean."

"You've always been…" She hesitated, trying to come up with the proper word. Controlling? Demanding? Overbearing? "Protective," she at last chose. "But lately I'm barely allowed to leave my rooms."

There was a brief silence, as if her father was debating whether he could dismiss her concern. Then, seeing her stubborn expression, he gave into the inevitable.

"There is some trouble with the corporation that funds my research," he slowly admitted.

Bianca nodded. She'd sensed a growing tension over the past few months, but her father had refused to acknowledge there was anything going on. It was a relief to have him at least assure her that she wasn't imagining things.

"What sort of trouble?" she pressed.

"I am not allowed to reveal the actual details, but there has been some violence directed toward a few laboratories and several death threats," he said.

Her eyes widened. Okay. Now she understood why her father was so on edge.

"That's terrible," she breathed.

"I am sure this is just a temporary disturbance, but until it passes I would prefer that you remain in the house," he continued in smooth tones.

"I…" She bit back her protest. Her father was only trying to keep her safe. "Very well."

The smile returned. "I promise that we will take a trip to Phoenix when I return from Florida," he said.

With the proverbial pat on the head offered, Joshua turned to leave the room, clearly confident she would obey his command.

And why wouldn't he be confident?

She'd always been an obedient daughter, choosing submission over her inner urge to rock the boat.

Heaving a frustrated sigh, Bianca wandered across the tiled floor and glanced out the French doors. She was in time to witness her father leave the house and step into the waiting car.

He never glanced back. Or checked to see if she was waving good-bye. Joshua Ford was a man who was always focused on his goals.

Still feeling tense, Bianca headed toward the back of the house. After she'd turned eighteen, her father had built on a private suite that overlooked the back pool.

It was a lovely space designed in pale blue and silver. It had a living room, a large bedroom, and an en-suite bathroom.

Stepping through the double doors that led to the apartment, Bianca came to a sharp halt.

She could sense someone. She didn't know how. Or why. But she was absolutely certain that there was an intruder nearby.

"Hello?" Reaching out she fumbled to flick on the light switch. Instantly the room was bathed with a soft glow. She frowned, glancing around the space that held a sofa and matching chairs, with low coffee tables that held lovely pottery she bought from the local Indian tribe. "Is someone there? Donald?"

She stepped forward, the hair on her nape prickling. Was she imagining…

Her thoughts were scattered when a hand suddenly slammed over her mouth while an arm wrapped around her waist. With a shocking speed she felt a hard body pressed against her back as warm lips brushed the top of her ear.

"I don't want to hurt you, but I will if you scream or try to escape," a husky male voice warned. "Nod if you understand."

Panic exploded through her, but she maintained enough sense to give a nod of her head. She could actually feel the ruthless steel of his muscles. There was no way in hell she would be able to fight her way free. She had to stall for time. Either for the chance to escape or for one of the bodyguards to come and check on her.

Slowly lowering his hand from her mouth, he turned her to face him.

Bianca gasped. Not in fear. In fact, the looming hysteria was forgotten as she gazed at the intruder in mindless shock.

Holy crap. She felt as if she'd been sucker-punched. He was just so…flawless.

His lean, bronzed face looked like it'd been chiseled by the hand of an artist. The dark hair that was sexily mussed matched the goatee that framed his lush lips. And his eyes held a golden heat that she would swear she could feel searing over her skin.

But it wasn't just his stunning beauty. Or the intense male energy that crackled through the air.

It was the sensation that this stranger had stepped straight out of her deepest fantasy. As if they'd been destined for one another since the beginning of time.

Which meant that she was either going insane, or the stress of being confronted by a dangerous invader was befuddling her poor brain.

The man stared at her in silence, his gaze taking a slow inventory of her stiff body before returning to meet her bewildered gaze.

"Who are you?" he rasped.

"Bianca Ford," she breathed.

His brows snapped together, his nose flaring as if her name had somehow offended him.

"You're Joshua Ford's wife?"

"No." She shook her head. So he wasn't just a random intruder. He knew her father. Or at least he knew this was her father's house. "His daughter."

He continued to glare at her, but she could almost sense a portion of his outrage ease.

"Where is he?" he demanded.

Bianca briefly considered lying, only to give a small shrug.

Her father traveled to Miami several times a month. It wasn't exactly a secret.

"He's flying to Florida."

There was something that sounded like a low growl that rumbled deep in his chest.

"Don't lie to me."

She blinked, wondering why it suddenly felt so hot. "I'm not. I swear it's the truth."

Clearly the man had expected to find Joshua at home. "Shit. When will he be back?"

"I don't know. He's usually gone a few days. Sometimes a week." She licked her dry lips. "Who are you?"

"I'm the one asking the questions," he snapped.

Her spine stiffened. He was stunningly gorgeous, and she couldn't deny that there was a part of her that remained weirdly captivated by his presence.

But he was also a jerk.

The sooner one of the guards came to rescue her the better.

"If you'll tell me what you want, maybe I can help. Is it money?" she demanded. "I can open the safe."

He jerked, as if offended she might think he was a common thief.

"I have no need for your money."

"Then what?"

His lips parted, but before he could speak, his head was swiveling toward the door she'd left open.

"Who's that?"

It took a minute for her to catch the sound of approaching footsteps. Yeesh. She'd thought that she had good hearing. This man must have the ears of a bat.

"I assume that it's Donald," she said.

Again he stiffened, his eyes flashing with a strange glow. "Your husband?"

She shook her head. Why was he so anxious to assume she was married?

"I don't have a husband," she said. "Donald's my bodyguard."

He stepped toward her, wrapping her in the warm scent of his skin. It was rich and musky, and it sent odd tingles through the center of her body.

"Why would you need a bodyguard?" he asked.

She sucked in a deep breath, the tantalizing musk making it difficult to think.

What was wrong with her?

"My father's a little overprotective," she admitted in distracted tones.

He studied her with an unnerving intensity. "Is he?"

"I suppose most father's feel the need to keep their daughters safe," she babbled.

"He must love you very much," he murmured.

Did he love her? It was the second time that night that Bianca found herself considering the question. And once again, she fiercely told herself that he must care for his only child. After all, he spent a fortune providing her with a comfortable home and plenty of food, plus an expensive education.

"I...yes, of course he does," she forced herself to say.

A sudden smile curled his lips. A smile that didn't reach his glowing eyes.

"Let's put that to the test."

She frowned. "What do you mean?"

"We're taking a trip together."

"What?" She took a hasty step back. "I'm not going anywhere with you."

His smile widened, revealing pearly white teeth. "It wasn't an invitation."

Fear returned, thundering through her as she tried to scramble away. "No."

Moving forward, the stranger reached out to wrap his arms around her. Then, with fluid ease, he scooped her off her feet and headed toward the French doors.

"Easy, female," he murmured as she pressed against his chest and kicked her feet. "I'm not going to hurt you."

It was insane, but she believed him. Perhaps because it was obvious he intended to use her as some sort of bargaining chip against her father. Or perhaps because she still couldn't shake the sensation that he was more than just a stranger.

And it was even more insane that the reason she was struggling was out of fear of what was going to happen to him if he carried out his impulsive plan to leave the house carrying her.

"The guards will shoot you if you try to kidnap me," she warned. "If you put me down and go away, I won't tell them about you until you've escaped."

* * * *

Was she worried about him?

The thought was disturbing as hell.

Almost as disturbing as the sweet scent of honey that clung to her creamy, satin skin.

Kayden released a low growl and forced himself to continue forward, refusing to glance down at the female who was threatening to ruin all his plans.

Christ. Nothing was going like it was supposed to.

He'd come here to hunt down Joshua Ford and kill him. Instead, he'd discovered that Joshua was out of state and this gentle, disturbingly lovely female was his only hope of achieving his revenge.

Or at least he told himself she was his only hope. How else could he excuse his decision to carry her off like some damned pirate claiming his booty rather than chasing down the bastard who'd murdered his parents?

Furious with his fierce reaction to a female who was the daughter of his enemy, he glared down at her wide, vulnerable eyes.

"You try to attract the attention of the guards and I'll kill them," he snarled, opening the glass door to step onto the patio that surrounded the pool.

She scowled, even as she halted her struggles. "Are you always so violent?"

"You have no idea, princess," he muttered, trying to ignore his inner puma who was already obsessed with the thought of licking and nibbling that creamy skin from head to toe.

She made a sound of frustration. "My name is Bianca, not princess."

"Ssh," he ordered, sliding through the shadows, his night vision allowing him to move as if it was bright daylight.

Clearly worried that he would make good on his threat, Bianca remained silent as he tightened his hold on her and leaped over the stone wall that surrounded the estate.

She sucked in a shocked breath. Whether it was because of his leap that should have revealed he was something other than human, or because she realized he was serious about kidnapping her, he didn't know.

He jogged over the hard, packed ground, heading directly toward the truck he'd left running behind a large swell of rocks and dirt.

Leaning forward, he pulled open the door and settled her in the passenger seat, careful to wrap the belt around her.

Not because he feared she might run. He could always catch her. But he wasn't willing to risk having her fragile, human body injured in case they were in a wreck.

Why he cared wasn't something he wanted to think about.

Rounding the hood, he took his own seat and switched on the engine. Then, not bothering with the headlights, he stomped his foot on the gas.

"Where are you taking me?" she demanded as they bounced over the dips and swells.

Kayden ground his teeth. That was the question, wasn't it?

He couldn't take her back to the Wildlands. Not when he intended to lure Joshua back to Arizona. But he couldn't stay in the middle of the desert.

What he needed was someplace he could hide Bianca, and yet be close enough to strike when Joshua returned.

It came to him like a strike of lightning. He knew the perfect place.

"Just sit quietly," he commanded, heading directly toward the nearby highway. "And if you try to escape—"

"Yeah, I know," she interrupted. "You'll kill me."

Kayden hid his grimace, allowing a silence to fill the truck. It was ridiculous to feel a pang of regret that he was forced to terrify her. After all, her father was a butcher who'd destroyed his life. And from the files he had uncovered, his parents weren't the only Pantera he'd used in his sick experiments.

This female was the spawn of the devil.

Unfortunately, his cat refused to agree with his human heart.

It was prowling beneath his skin, urgently wanting to be released so it could rub against the female, coating her in his musk.

Almost as if...

With a silent curse, Kayden slammed the door on his dangerous thoughts.

Soon enough he would send a message to Joshua Ford, demanding a meeting. Once he had his hands on the man, he would release Bianca and she could return to her home. That would be the end of it.

Repeating the words over and over, they'd driven nearly an hour when she abruptly spoke.

"Are you at least going to tell me your name?" she asked, her voice strained as if she was struggling to contain her fear.

"Kayden," he grudgingly offered.

"Do you work for my father?"

He released a sharp laugh. "Not hardly."

She turned her head, her golden tresses escaping the scrunchie to tumble over her shoulders.

"Then why are you so angry with him?"

His brows drew together as he shot her a curious glance. "How do you know I'm angry?"

"I can feel it." She held up her slender hands. "I know it sounds silly, but I've always been able to sense emotions."

A wild, crazy idea drifted on the edges of his mind.

Was it possible that she was one of them?

No. If she had Pantera blood he would be able to smell it in her. Not to mention being able to sense her cat.

Right?

Of course, Joshua Ford was a scientist who'd spent years experimenting with Pantera blood and DNA. The Goddess only knew what he'd done to his own daughter.

"Tell me about yourself," he abruptly demanded.

She blinked at the edge in his voice. "Why?"

He shrugged. "It will pass the time."

She hesitated, clearly aware that he was digging for something.

"There's nothing to tell," she finally muttered.

Kayden glanced in the rearview mirror, ensuring that no one was following. He didn't doubt that Bianca's absence had been noticed and a frantic search was already being organized.

"What about your parents?"

She sent him a confused glance. "My father's a doctor who is researching a cure for cancer."

Seriously? That was his cover story?

"For Benson Enterprises?" he asked.

Her confusion deepened. "There's a Christopher Benson listed on the board of directors, but my father works for Cruise Clinic and Laboratory."

Kayden's jaw tightened. Christopher Benson was the man at the center of the evil. A true monster who Kayden fully intended to kill.

After he was done with Joshua Ford.

"And your father researches cancer?" he asked.

"Yes," she said with absolute sincerity. She truly believed that's what her father did. "He actually cured me when I was just a child."

Ah. So she'd undergone treatment. So what the hell had Joshua been doing to her?

"Really?"

She frowned at his blatant disbelief. "Yes, really."

He didn't press her. It was obvious she had no idea what her father might or might not have been doing to her during her treatments.

"And your mother?" he instead asked.

"She died when I was just a baby."

Died or was killed? Kayden was aware that Benson had been impregnating Pantera females with human sperm.

"Was she a scientist?"

A deep sadness rippled over her expressive face. "I don't know much about her," she admitted. "It's too painful for my father to discuss her, so I stopped asking questions."

"What about brothers or sisters?"

"None." She shook her head. "It's just me and my father."

Kayden gave a low grunt, falling back into silence. He didn't have any proof that this female was anything more than the daughter of Joshua Ford, but he was growingly convinced that there was something different about her.

Or maybe he just wanted to think that she was more than a mere human.

"Are you going to tell me why you kidnapped me?" she demanded.

"No."

His sharp refusal tightened her lips, and with a loud huff she folded her arms over her chest and glared out the side window.

Kayden gave a small shake of his head, breathing deep of Bianca's honey scent that drenched the air.

What the hell had he gotten himself into?

Chapter Three

Bianca was determined to remain silent. If her annoying captor didn't want to tell her what was going on, then fine. She wouldn't talk.

After all, her father would soon track her down.

She had every confidence that he would use his considerable power and money to organize a search that would be capable of finding her within a few hours.

But as soon as they entered the fringes of town, she easily forgot her determined pledge of silence.

"Oh," she breathed, her eyes wide as she took in the familiar skyline and the silhouette of a towering Ferris wheel. Not that she'd ever been to the bustling city. But even she'd seen it on TV. "This is Vegas, isn't it?"

Kayden sent her a startled glance. "You've never been here before?"

She shook her head. "My father occasionally takes me to Phoenix, but I spend most of my time at home."

Easily negotiating the traffic that was surprisingly heavy considering it had to be past nine o'clock, he continued to study her with blatant curiosity.

"You didn't attend school?"

"I had a private tutor when I was young and then I did my college courses online," she said, not surprised by his confusion.

She had an unconventional childhood.

"Is there a reason you've been so isolated?" he demanded.

"When I was young I had to be near the lab for my treatments," she explained.

"What sort of treatments?"

Bianca shrugged. There were huge chunks of her childhood that she could barely remember. And even now, she had only bits and pieces of memory from her time in the clinic.

There was always a narrow hospital bed. And straps that held her down so she wouldn't injure herself. And a bright light overhead that always felt like it was burning a hole in her brain.

And pain.

Lots of pain.

"I'm not exactly sure," she told him. "It's still in the experimental stage."

He made a sound of disbelief. "You don't know what was done to you?"

She hunched a shoulder. He made her feel as if she'd been an idiot not to constantly question her father on every detail of the drugs being used on her.

Clearly he hadn't spent his life with death as a constant companion.

When she wasn't actually receiving her treatments she didn't want to think about them. She wanted to pretend she was a normal woman with a long future stretching ahead of her.

"I was usually sedated during the hours I had to be at the clinic," she said.

"And now?" he asked.

"Now what?"

"Do you still get treatments?"

She nodded. "Once a week."

"Is there anyone else receiving the experimental cure?"

She frowned. He sounded as if he didn't believe that her father was a renowned scientist who was making a huge difference in the world.

"Of course, although I never see them," she said, her voice sharp. Whatever her feelings for Joshua Ford, she didn't doubt his determination to keep her alive and well. "My father is trying to get the drugs approved by the FDA, so he has to take care that each of our treatments are individually documented and there's no chance of cross-contamination."

"Hmm."

She shook her head. There was no point in arguing. He clearly had something against her father. He was never going to accept that he was just trying to help her.

Leaning her forehead against the side window, she lost herself in the beauty of the vivid lights and flashing neon signs. The town was bright and brash and seething with an energy that she could tangibly feel pulsing deep inside her.

She loved it.

Of course, it didn't matter how distracted she was by her circus-like surroundings, she remained acutely aware of the man at her side.

The heat of him seemed to reach out and wrap around her. His warm, musky scent teased at her nose. And the gravitational force of his male sensuality threatened to suck her in like a black hole consuming everything in its path.

Turning off the main strip, Kayden pulled the truck into a parking lot at the back of a large hotel.

She glanced toward him in surprise. She'd expected him to drive through the city on their way to…where she didn't know, but she'd assumed it would be isolated. Wasn't that what most kidnappers would do?

"Is this where we're staying?" she asked.

"Yes." Shutting off the engine, he jumped out of the truck and headed around the hood. Then, pulling open her door, he unbuckled her seat belt. "I prefer to let you walk on your own, but if you fight me I'll have to carry you."

She glared at him, not nearly as afraid as she should be. "You don't think that would attract attention?"

He shrugged. "This is Vegas."

Okay. He probably had a point. Swiveling to the side, she climbed out of the truck, taking care not to brush against his lean body. She had a feeling that his mere touch would send her up in flames.

Kayden seemed to be taking the same care to avoid an accidental touch, leading her toward a small service door. Pausing to open a silver box that was built into the wide jamb, he placed his hand against an electronic scanner. The door slid open to reveal the inside of an elevator.

Bianca lifted her brows as she entered the stainless steel cab and watched Kayden press the button for the top floor. She might not be familiar with Vegas, but she did know this wasn't how most guests entered the hotel.

In fact, she suspected there was something very top secret about this entrance.

There was a shudder of movement as they were swept upward at a speed that made her head spin. Then, before she could catch her breath, the doors swooshed open and she was stepping directly into a penthouse suite.

She blinked, then blinked again as she unconsciously moved forward. She was distantly aware that she was in a large sitting room with plush gray furniture and a polished black floor. The coffee tables were glass and chrome, with expensive prints framed in silver and hung around the room.

Her attention, however, was locked on the glass wall that offered a panoramic view of the strip.

"Good. God," she breathed. "This is stunning." She turned her head to discover her companion was standing a few feet away, his arms folded over his chest as he studied her with an odd expression. "Have you stayed here before?" she demanded.

"A few times," he admitted.

Her head tilted to the side. "Do you do business in Vegas?"

His lips twisted. "Nice try." With a sharp shake of his head he was pulling out a cell phone and heading across the room. "I have a call to make. Behave yourself."

She watched as he disappeared down a hallway that she suspected led to the bedrooms. A strange shiver of anticipation inched down her spine, while that restlessness returned to curl through her abdomen.

Her entire body tingled with the urge to follow Kayden and tumble him onto the nearest bed. Then, she wanted to lick him from head to toe.

Insanity…

Giving a sharp shake of her head, she headed back across the room. Obviously, she needed some time away from the man to clear away the crazy.

Studying the high-tech instrument panel next to the elevator, she at last copied Kayden's method by laying her hand against the screen built into the wall.

Instantly the doors opened and she stepped inside.

A faint smile curved her lips. Kayden had told her to behave herself, but he hadn't said anything about staying in the room.

Hitting the button for the lobby, she braced her feet as she dropped at an alarming speed.

She wasn't sure what she intended to do. A part of her knew that any reasonable woman would try to escape. It didn't matter that she didn't have her phone or any ID. If she could find a cop she could tell them that she'd been kidnapped. Once they contacted her father they would realize she wasn't some insane person and take her to safety.

But even as the doors to the elevator slid open and she stepped into the busy lobby made of marble floors and fluted columns, she knew she wasn't going to find the nearest police officer.

She could tell herself that she was afraid that if she alerted her father that Kayden might hurt him. After all, it was obvious that he'd come to the house expecting to find him. And that he'd taken her with the hope that he could use her to reach Joshua Ford.

Or she could pretend that she simply wanted a few hours of freedom from her father's smothering need to protect her. He would never, ever allow her to spend time in Vegas. And certainly he would never let her mingle among a crowd of strangers like she was just a normal tourist.

But the truth was…she wanted to spend time with Kayden.

It didn't make any sense.

He was a stranger who'd snuck into her home and kidnapped her. He might very well prove to be a threat to her father.

Hell, he might be a threat to her.

But there was a part of her that refused to dismiss the sense that she'd been destined to meet the aggravating, gorgeous man. And that he was fated to be a part of her future.

Crossing the marble floor, Bianca entered the darkened casino and was instantly besieged with sensations.

Not only the loud clamor of people and dinging machines, or the sound of music blaring from one of the numerous bars. It was the overwhelming barrage of emotions.

Pleasure, excitement, desperation.

Shivering, Bianca wandered past the slot machines, and then the velvet-covered tables where people threw dice while onlookers cheered or groaned with each toss.

Most of the emotions washed over her like a wave, but there was one that actually tugged at her. Almost as if the person was calling her name.

Compelled forward, she dodged past a group of drunken men who were intent on capturing her attention and headed toward a service door nearly hidden beside the bathrooms. Hesitating only a second, she entered the stairwell and quickly jogged up the steps to a steel door at the top. Pushing it open, she found herself standing on top of a flat roof.

The late night breeze tugged at her hair that had come loose from her ponytail and cut through her thin sweater. Wrapping her arms around her waist, she cautiously moved across the tarred shingles. The sense of despair that had been calling to her was almost deafening, battering against her with an intensity she hadn't expected.

Stepping around a large air-conditioning unit, she at last caught sight of the cause of the emotional avalanche.

A young woman stood on the edge of the roof, her slender body wearing nothing more than a skimpy waitress outfit and her pale face turned upward, as if seeking an answer to her problem from the heavens.

"Don't," she called out, sensing the woman a breath away from jumping.

The woman impulsively took a step back before turning to send Bianca a furious glare.

"Stay away."

Pretending she didn't know what was going on, Bianca lifted her hands and continued to inch forward. She wanted to get close enough she could grab the young woman if worse came to worse.

"You're standing too close to the edge," she said. "You might fall."

The woman reached up to angrily brush aside the tears that stained her pale face. She had blonde hair that was going dark at the roots and dark eyes that were bloodstained. As if she'd been crying for hours.

"Are you an idiot?" the woman snapped. "I'm standing here because I want to fall."

Bianca took another step forward. "Why?"

The woman bit her bottom lip. "Because I can't take any more."

Bianca grimaced, her heart twisting. "I feel your pain."

The woman released an angry breath. "Dammit. I'm sick of hearing that. No one can feel my pain."

"No, I really can," Bianca said, close enough to reach out and lightly touch the woman's arm. "It's a gift I was born with."

The woman continued to glare at her, but she didn't pull away. "Feelings aren't a gift. They're a curse."

"Some days they are," Bianca agreed, allowing her fingers to trace up the woman's shoulder in a soothing motion. She'd discovered she had a strange ability to offer comfort with her touch. Even her burly bodyguards had mentioned that they felt better after she gave them a hug. "But the wonderful thing is that while they can cause us distress, they also bring us our greatest joy."

The woman sniffed, her tears drying as she gave a hesitant shake of her head.

"Not tonight."

"No, not tonight." Taking care not to startle her, Bianca wrapped an arm around her waist and urged her toward the center of the roof. "But the dark will pass and the sun will rise. You just have to give it time."

For long moments the woman leaned heavily against Bianca, her head nestled on Bianca's shoulder. Then, sucking in a deep breath, she slowly straightened and looked around. The blank expression that had been settled on her pretty face was slowly replaced by one of horror.

Clearly she was realizing where she was, and what she'd nearly done.

"Oh my God," she rasped, shaking her head. "I don't know what I was thinking."

Bianca tried not to stiffen as she felt a sizzling heat flare down her back. At the same time the—well, whatever it was deep inside her that seemed connected to Kayden—was stirred to life.

He was on the roof. And approaching from behind.

"You're safe," she murmured, trying to concentrate on the woman shivering in her arms.

"I almost did it," the woman breathed. "I truly wanted to end it all."

"It's okay," she said in soft tones, her hand continuing to rub up and down her arm.

The woman lifted her head, her face as pale as the moonlight that spilled over the roof. "Thank you. Thank you. I—" The woman's eyes widened as she caught sight of the man walking toward them. "Oh. I have to go."

Darting away, the woman headed toward the opposite side of the roof.

Bianca watched until she disappeared from sight before she slowly turned. Tiny bursts of excitement raced through her as she discovered the tall, fiercely beautiful man standing only inches away, his eyes glowing with cognac fire.

God almighty. Lust thundered through her. A new, ferocious hunger that she feared wasn't going to go away.

Not unless…

She licked her dry lips

* * * *

Kayden studied the female who was surely destined to drive him nuts.

Dammit. He'd gone into the privacy of the bedroom to make his call to Joshua Ford. Not only because he didn't want Bianca to overhear his conversation with her father, but because he needed space to think.

Being near Bianca was beginning to cloud his brain.

The slender temptation of her body. The vulnerable sweetness in her eyes. The sweet honey scent that made his puma growl with need.

He'd never dreamed she could actually get out of the suite. After all, it was custom designed for Pantera. Which meant the security locks shouldn't open for anyone who wasn't a puma-shifter.

Or had the blood of a puma-shifter.

Furious with himself for risking everything, he'd jumped into the elevator and headed down. He hadn't needed to follow Bianca's scent. He'd been able to sense her. Which only increased his fury.

He could pretend that he'd kidnapped her to punish her father. And to even act as if the throbbing awareness was nothing more than mere lust. She was a beautiful woman. He was a healthy guy with a normal sexual appetite.

But there was nothing that could explain why his cat was bonding with her on a spiritual level.

The puma was trying to mate.

His anger had lasted until he'd entered the casino and seen her wandering through the crowd. She hadn't been trying to escape. Or even to capture the attention of the numerous security guards.

Instead, it looked as if she'd been captivated by her surroundings, her gaze darting around the noisy crowd as she'd moved deeper into the vast room.

Kayden had followed in her wake, unwilling to steal her moment of wonder. Then, she'd been angling straight toward a back door, as if she was on a mission. He'd followed behind, telling himself he had to make sure she wasn't going to slip away. Or that she wasn't in contact with her father.

The last thing he'd expected was to witness her save a young woman's life.

Any hope that he could treat her as nothing more than a bargaining chip was forever gone.

"I wondered where you were hiding," he said, his tone rough as he struggled against the urge to sweep her in his arms and carry her back to the penthouse.

Predictably, her chin tilted to a defiant angle. She might be innocent and vulnerable, but she had a spirit that would refuse to ever let him dominate her. At least not on an intellectual level. On a physical level he had high hopes it would be a whole other story.

His cat purred in approval.

"I wasn't hiding," she said.

"I told you to stay in the suite."

"No," she countered. "You told me to behave myself."

He thinned his lips to hide his sudden urge to smile. "Hmm. I'll remember that." He tilted his head to the side. "How did you get the door unlocked?"

She shrugged. "I placed my hand on the screen and it opened."

It was obvious she had no idea just how extraordinary her feat had been. His lips parted to explain, only to pause.

The anger toward her father still flowed through his body like acid. It warned him to say nothing that could be used against his people if he decided to return her to her home.

Then he gave a small shrug.

There was no way he was letting this female go.

Not only because he suspected that she was more Pantera than human, but because his puma wasn't going to allow her to walk away.

End of story.

"That shouldn't have been possible," he said, holding her wary gaze. "Not unless you're a Pantera."

He could feel her sudden tension, as if she already sensed he was about to shake the very foundations of her world.

"I don't understand," she muttered.

Unable to resist temptation, Kayden reached out to lightly cup her cheek with his hand. Desire punched through him. Her skin was as milky soft as he'd suspected and warm to his touch despite the cool breeze.

Far warmer than the skin of a human.

She might not be a full Pantera, but she certainly had some of their blood.

"You've heard of Pantera?" he asked.

"Yes. They're puma shifters who live in the bayous of Louisiana," she said, her brows drawing together. "Are you one?"

He nodded. "I am."

"Oh." Her gaze skimmed over his face, as if looking for some sign that he wasn't human.

His thumb absently brushed her full lower lip, the animal inside him pacing with a restless hunger.

"Does that scare you?"

She shrugged. "I've already been kidnapped. There's not much more that you could do to me."

He made a sound of disbelief before he was abruptly wrapping her in his arms around her waist and pulling her hard against his body. Then, lowering his head, he pressed his face into the curve of her neck.

"So innocent," he muttered, glad she couldn't see all the things he wanted to do to her. Not that he would hurt her...but he was a male who enjoyed the scrape of fangs and the gentle kiss of claws during sex.

She shivered, her hands lifting to rest against his chest.

"Kayden, what are you doing?"

He sucked in a deep breath, his blood pumping at the sweet scent of honey. Dear Goddess, he wanted to lap her up.

His tongue stroked a rough path down her throat, his cock stiffening as he wondered if her taste would be just as addictive between her legs.

"Trying to figure out what the hell you are," he groaned.

Her nails dug into his sweater, her body arching in an unconscious invitation.

"I'm just a woman—"

"No," he interrupted. "There's more than that. You shouldn't have been able to open that door."

She trembled, the scent of her arousal spicing the air. She was no more immune to the potent chemistry between them than he was.

"You must have forgotten to lock it."

He slowly lifted his head, staring deep into her wide eyes.

"And the way that you eased that female's pain."

She licked her lips, a habit that was making him insane with the need to cover those lips in a kiss of sheer desperation.

"She just needed someone to listen," Bianca protested.

"No, she needed a healer," he told her.

She stilled, studying him with a spark of interest that she couldn't hide.

"A healer?"

"My people are born with specific talents," he explained, not going into the full details of how the Elders could sense the spark in each of them. "Some are Hunters. They're our warriors. Some are Diplomats, which include the Geeks—"

"You call them geeks?" she abruptly demanded.

He chuckled at her expression. Clearly she thought it was an insult.

"Trust me, princess, we claim the title with pride."

"You're one of them?"

"Yes." His hands absently rubbed up and down her back, savoring the feel of her slender curves. She fit against him with a perfection that had everything to do with fate. "My specialty is creating programs that can retrieve miniscule amounts of computer data and turn it back into a readable file. Like a scientist taking a tiny amount of DNA and being able to duplicate it until they have a full human profile." He abruptly grimaced, realizing he was bragging as if he was a cub trying to impress his childhood sweetheart. Yeesh. What had this female done to him? "And we have Healers," he continued, finally getting to the point. "They're capable of using their powers to ease wounds, whether they're physical or emotional."

Her frown deepened, as if a part of her was trying to reject what he was telling her.

"What does that have to do with me?" she at last demanded.

"You have Pantera blood," he said in clear, concise tones. "There's no other explanation."

"No."

Although he was prepared for her shocked disbelief, he hadn't anticipated the frantic struggle to escape.

Briefly his arms tightened around her, holding her close. He couldn't let her flee when she was clearly upset.

But as she pounded her fists against his chest and tried to kick at his shins, he reluctantly allowed his arms to drop. She wasn't hurting him, but she was going to injure herself if she continued to batter at him.

Once out of his grip, she turned and ran toward the door. Almost as if the very devil was on her heels.

Shit. Kayden heaved a sigh, shoving his fingers through his hair.

That could have gone better.

Chapter Four

Joshua Ford was just stepping into the veranda of the sprawling mansion built on the fringes of Miami when the call came through.

He listened in silence as the unknown man gave him orders to meet him in the desert outside of Vegas. Then, pocketing the cellphone, he considered his options.

They were limited.

Far more limited than he was accustomed to.

After all, he was a man who had a strategy for every emergency. And usually more than one. There was a plan *A*, plan *B*, and plan *C*.

How else could he ensure that his clinic was the most successful of all of the Benson Enterprise laboratories?

His dedication to detail had at last started to pay off.

Not only had the innermost circle that surrounded the head of the corporation, Christopher Benson, started to crumble beneath the strain of the past few months, but his own research in using Pantera DNA to cure human diseases had at last started to gain the attention it deserved.

Everything was perfect.

And then he'd received the call and he realized that his assumption that he was incapable of being caught off guard was nothing more than sheer arrogance. The damned Pantera had not only invaded his home, but he'd managed to strike where Joshua was most vulnerable.

With a shake of his head, Joshua gestured toward one of the uniformed guards that was standing next to the heavy double doors leading into the house.

The man hurried forward. "Yes, sir?"

"I need you to give my apologies to Mr. Benson," he said in clipped tones. "And call the airport to tell them to prepare the jet."

The guard blinked, obviously hired for his skill with a gun and not his intelligence.

"The jet?" he muttered in confusion. "You just arrived."

Joshua's lips thinned. "I'm aware of that."

"But—"

The man's protest was cut short as one of the doors was pulled open and the shadowed outline of a thin male form was revealed.

"Is there a problem?"

Joshua felt a chill inch down his spine. Although he'd been traveling more and more to Miami to deliver the serum that Christopher used to increase his lifespan, he rarely met with the older man. Now he struggled not to look away from the ravages on the thin face caused by time and disease.

Once Christopher took the serum, he would once again look like a robust, middle-aged man, but for now it was difficult to meet him eye to eye.

"Nothing I can't handle," he murmured. He'd sacrificed everything to become Benson's most trusted researcher. There was no way in hell he was going to let this bump in the road threaten his ultimate goal

There was the sound of a harsh, rattling breath. "Those are the exact words that Stanton used before he ended up dead and yet another of my valuable assets was invaded by the Pantera."

Joshua forced a stiff smile to his lips. Stanton had once been treated as Benson's prodigal son. The man had been given everything. Money. Stature. Power. All the things that Joshua lusted after.

Now he was dumped in an unmarked grave.

An ignoble fate that Joshua had no intention of sharing.

"Stanton might have been loyal, but he never possessed the proper ambition," he said with a well-rehearsed confidence.

"And you do?" Christopher wheezed, leaning on a cane he clutched in one skeleton hand.

Joshua held up the small cooler that contained the vials of serum. "Do you doubt me?"

Christopher gave a snap of his fingers and instantly the guard reached out to take the container.

"I have been disappointed too many times in the past," the older man continued to complain. "At this moment I doubt everyone. Including you."

"I have never disappointed you," he murmured.

Christopher made a petulant sound. "I'm disappointed that you're running off."

Joshua nodded toward the cooler. "I did bring the serum, as requested. I'm certain one of your private nurses can administer the necessary dosage."

"I wanted to discuss bringing your daughter to Miami."

"Bianca?" Joshua stiffened. "Why?"

"Our military contracts have temporarily dried up. I need another source of funding to keep my numerous clinics open," Christopher rasped. "Your daughter's miraculous cure from cancer will provide us with a way to convince the pharmaceutical companies to invest in Benson Enterprises."

Another chill inched down Joshua's spine. This one far worse.

A part of him had always known this was a risk.

But as he'd developed methods of using the Pantera blood to create various drugs, he'd hoped that his cure of Bianca would be forgotten.

"I assure you I am not running off," he said in smooth tones. "There has been a slight problem at home. The sooner I deal with it, the sooner I can return."

Christopher hadn't lived as long as he had and developed an underworld empire without a cunning intelligence and the ability to read people.

"Hmm. Now why do I sense that this slight problem is far more serious than you're willing to admit?" the older man demanded.

Despite his casual air, Joshua was already counting the cost of failure.

"As I said, I will handle it," he promised, backing his way off the terrace.

"Be sure that you do. I'm at the end of my patience, Joshua," Christopher snapped. "Bad things are likely to happen if I'm disappointed again."

"I understand," Joshua muttered, turning on his heel to hurry toward the waiting car.

Shit.

As much as he hated acting on impulse, he had no choice but to meet with the Pantera without organizing a proper plan. And worse, he was going to have to pray that he could kill two birds with one stone.

* * * *

Bianca didn't know where she was going.

Not until she entered the penthouse suite and crossed to stare out the glass wall.

This time she didn't bother to wonder why she wasn't making more of an effort to flee from her captor. Not when she knew deep inside that he had answers she needed to hear.

After all, she would be a liar if she didn't admit that she always knew there was something different about her. Not only her ability to feel emotions, but the knowledge that she could hear better and see better, and even smell better than any of her trained guards.

And there was that restless sense that a part of her was…waiting. She didn't know what she was waiting for, but she recognized immediately it had something to do with Kayden.

That didn't mean, however, that she was ready to be reasonable.

Not when her entire world was being turned upside down.

Spinning around, she pressed her back against the smoky glass, her heart forgetting to beat as she watched Kayden prowl toward her. God almighty. He was so gorgeous. His lean, perfect features. His smoldering cognac eyes. His hair that her fingers itched to run through.

And that musky scent. It was seeping into her like the finest aphrodisiac, making her think of soft sheets and his hard body sliding over her naked flesh.

"Stay back," she warned.

He came to an instant halt, his hands lifting in a gesture of peace.

"I'm not going to hurt you."

"You said that before and then you threaten to do all sorts of bad things when you want to order me around," she reminded him.

Guilt flared through his eyes. "I didn't know."

"Know what?" she demanded.

"That you were one of us."

She shook her head. "I'm not." The denial sounded hollow, even to herself. "And it shouldn't matter anyway. I wouldn't want you hurt just because you're a Pantera."

He studied her in silence for a long, nerve-wracking moment.

"I recently discovered that my parents were killed by humans, and not in a plane accident as I originally thought," he abruptly admitted. "It's been difficult to adjust to the revelation."

A renegade of sympathy flared through her. It was obvious that he'd loved his parents very much.

"I'm sorry for your loss, I really am," she said. "But that doesn't give you the right to act like a—"

"A jackass?" he suggested when words failed her.

"Yes."

He stepped toward her, an expression that was impossible to read on his beautiful male features.

"Can we talk?"

"Talk about what?"

"You know."

She hunched her shoulder. "Why are you doing this?"

"Asking you to talk?"

She glared at him with impatience. "Trying to confuse me."

"How could I do that?" He took another step forward. And then another.

She shivered. She tried to tell herself it was fear. Standing so close to him, there was a lethal edge to him that had nothing to do with his hard muscles and silky smooth movements. But fear didn't explain the curl of excitement through the pit of her stomach or the ache between her legs.

"Kidnapping me," she tried to bluff. "Taking me to this place. Claiming I'm not who I think I am."

His eyes darkened as if he could actually sense the arousal that was shuddering through her.

"Who do you think you are?" he asked, moving until his body was brushing against her, his hands cupping her shoulders.

"Nobody," she breathed, lost in the fierce glow of his eyes. "I'm nobody."

"A lie," he growled, burying his face in her neck. "I can't sense your cat, but I can tell that you have our blood."

She shivered, her mind clouding with a need that was swiftly becoming unbearable.

"That's impossible."

His lips skimmed down her throat, creating a path of erotic destruction. "I would have agreed with you just a few months ago. Either you were born a Pantera or a human."

Her hands lifted, laying against his chest. But she didn't push him away as she should have. Instead her head tilted back, offering him even greater access to her tender flesh.

"What changed?"

A low growl rumbled through the air. "Men like your father."

Her fingers curled, her nails digging into the soft fabric of his sweater. Her knees were weak, her heart lodged in her throat.

His lips felt hot enough to sear her skin, his sexual energy a vibrant, tangible force that sizzled through the air.

"I don't understand," she muttered. "What does my father have to do with this?"

The heat in the air was abruptly threaded with fury.

"Benson Enterprises has been kidnapping and experimenting with my people," he snarled, his lips nuzzling her frantic pulse that pounded at the base of her neck. "We don't know for how long, but we know without a doubt that there are humans who've been injected with Pantera blood as well as their DNA."

Injected with the blood of a puma-shifter? Or more disturbing, given their DNA? She struggled to think through the haze of sensual pleasure that was fogging her mind.

"And you think that's what has been done to me?"

He licked a rough tongue along the line of her collarbone.

"Yes."

Oh, lord. Pleasure jolted through her. "What would that mean?"

"It's hard to say for certain, but you would more than likely have a few of our gifts."

"I would surely know if I have a cat inside me?" she demanded.

"It's a little more complicated than that," he informed her, lifting his head to study her pale face with a brooding gaze. "But you wouldn't know for sure until I take you home. It takes the magic of the Wildlands to allow us to shift."

Bianca frowned. Until now, she'd been more bemused than terrified. It was possible that she hadn't fully absorbed what he was implying. Or maybe she was just happy to have an explanation for the oddities that had plagued her over the years.

But the thought of leaving everything she knew and being taken to Kayden's home was...

Well, she wasn't entirely sure. She just knew the intensity of her reaction was unnerving.

"I'm not going to the Wildlands," she protested. "You can't make me."

He grimaced, as if her words had actually struck a nerve.

"No. I won't make you, princess," he swore in low, husky tones. "You should feel free to do whatever you want."

Illogically, his promise didn't ease her strange emotions. Instead, she found herself feeling something perilously close to disappointment.

As if she wanted him to insist she had to travel with him to the Wildlands.

"I can return to my father?" she pressed.

His eyes darkened. "Is that what you want?"

No...

The word whispered through her very soul.

It might be disloyal to the man who'd raised her, but she didn't want to return to her isolated home to face a future of loneliness. Not when the alternative offered the potential to be close to Kayden.

Still, she had to be reasonable.

"I have to have my treatments," she said, unable to hide her regret.

His brows snapped together. "No."

"What?"

"We don't have human diseases," he told her. "You have too much Pantera blood to ever have had cancer."

She made a strangled sound as the world once again shifted beneath her feet. Her entire life had revolved around her disease and depending on her father to keep death at bay.

If he'd lied...

She gave a slow shake of her head. "Enough, Kayden," she rasped.

"You're right," he agreed with a rueful grimace, leaning down to brush a soft kiss over her lips. "It's late, princess. Why don't we sleep on it, and you can decide tomorrow what you want to do?"

Her mouth tingled, the taste of him lingering with a decadent promise of pleasure.

Swaying toward him, Bianca was caught off guard when he abruptly dropped his arms and stepped back, his lean features impossible to read.

"Where are you going?" she asked as he turned to head across the sitting room.

"I need a shower." He paused at the door leading to the short hall.

"You can take the master suite. I'll use the guest room."

Bianca bit her bottom lip, feeling as if a part of her was missing as Kayden disappeared from view.

It didn't matter that he'd kidnapped her. Or turned her world upside down. Or even that she barely knew him.

She'd lived in isolation for the past twenty-two years, allowing her father to have complete control over her life. He'd used her love, her gratitude, and her sense of duty to keep her caged.

Now she could physically feel his chains on her breaking away.

It was glorious.

But it wasn't enough.

There were still a thousand unanswered questions, including what Kayden wanted with her father, but suddenly none of it mattered.

Nope.

Tonight she had one goal. Period.

Chapter Five

Bianca hurried toward the guest bedroom, entering just in time to hear the shower switch on.

She paused, glancing around the room handsomely decorated in shades of gray and black. Then, with quick movements, she tugged off her clothes.

Entering the large bathroom, she crossed the mosaic-tiled floor to enter the shower stall that was large enough to fit a football team.

The air was filled with a humid steam that was mixed with the scent of bath gel and warm male skin. It wrapped around her like a welcoming blanket. Bianca trembled, her nipples beading in anticipation as Kayden turned to regard her with a wary gaze.

"Bianca." He reached to shut off the water. "Is something wrong?"

She shook her head, determinedly advancing even as he backed against the wall. In the muted light, his skin shimmered like bronze, his dark hair slicked from his beautiful face. This was a first for her. Nerves hummed through her, like an electric current. She couldn't believe her own daring. It was completely out of character for her. But tonight she wasn't going to give in to her inner fears. She was going to be bold. Daring.

"I want to be with you."

A groan was ripped from his throat, his eyes squeezing shut, as if in pain. "Let me dry off and I'll join you in the sitting room."

She gave another shake of her head. Then, moving until their bodies were just inches apart, she reached up to smooth her hands over his broad chest. She groaned, savoring the sensation of his muscles clenching beneath her bold caress.

"I like it better here."

His eyes opened, his fingers wrapping around her wrists, although he made no effort to pull her hands away.

"I'm not human, princess," he rasped. "And my cat wants you with a hunger that I'm finding hard to leash."

"Why would you leash it?" she asked, tantalized by the thought of his inner puma.

His eyes glowed, accentuating his warning that he possessed an animal just beneath the surface. Bianca shivered, knowing it was the cat that was studying her with a hunter's gaze.

"Do you know what you're doing?" he demanded, his expression twisting with extreme torment.

She leaned forward, pressing a path of kisses over the slick skin of his chest. His taste was hot and wild and addictive.

Yum.

"I know."

"You can't," he breathed, his voice rough as his intoxicating musk filled the air.

Bianca felt something stir deep inside her. Was there an animal prowling just below her skin?

The notion was as intriguing as it was unsettling.

"Why can't I?" she demanded. "I'm a grown woman. If I want to spend the night with a man, I will."

Unexpectedly, Kayden stiffened, as if her words had somehow offended him.

"Is that what I am?" he growled. "Just another man?"

She pulled back, baffled by his sudden anger. "What does that mean?"

He released a sigh, as if regretting his harsh words. "I realize it will sound crazy to you, but my cat is convinced that this is much more than a Vegas quickie."

Oh. Relief surged through her. He felt the same sense of destiny that she did.

Amazing.

She went on her tiptoes to brush her lips along the line of his stubborn jaw.

"I don't think it's crazy," she said in a husky voice. "I think this is one of the most special moments of my life."

She felt him shudder, his muscles clenched tight.

"How special?" he demanded.

Her lips twitched at the sheer male need to be told he was unique.

"Super special," she readily admitted, nipping the lobe of his ear. "Even if I don't know why you're so angry with my father."

Kayden swooped his head down, kissing her with an intensity that sent lightning bolts of need sizzling through her body. She gasped, clutching at his shoulders as her toes curled in the warm water pooling at their feet.

"I don't want to discuss Joshua Ford," he commanded against her lips. "Not tonight."

She caught the sensuous fullness of his lower lip between her teeth, chuckling with pleasure when he groaned in helpless need.

"What do you want to discuss?" she asked softly.

He made a sound of frustration, his eyes glowing with the power of his cat in the billowing steam.

"Bianca, you haven't had time to fully process everything that's happened," he said, the words clearly being forced past his lips. "Once you've had time to—"

"I told you that I know what I want," she interrupted, arching herself against his naked body. Her heart skipped a beat at the feel of his hard cock pressed against her lower stomach.

Her mouth went dry. He was so large. Not only long, but thick.

And hot.

As if it was designed to brand her, marking her as his possession.

"Why don't you believe me?" she demanded.

His hands gripped her hips, his fingers digging into her flesh as if he were caught between the urge to yank her closer and shove her away.

"I want this to be perfect," he breathed. "I don't want you waking up and regretting spending the night in my arms."

She allowed her fingers to skim over his shoulders and then up the curve of his throat. Her touch was tentative. It felt incredibly intimate to touch his neck, as if he was allowing her an opportunity that he rarely offered to anyone else.

"There won't be any regrets."

He tensed, his eyes dark with pain. "You can't be sure of that. I still haven't told you everything."

She studied his taut expression.

He wasn't confessing anything she didn't already suspect. She knew damned well that he was hiding things from her. But right now, she couldn't make herself care.

Not when her entire body felt as if it was on fire.

She threaded her fingers through his damp hair. It was something she'd longed to do since she first caught sight of him. Then she deliberately rubbed the tight buds of her breasts against his chest, groaning at the tiny darts of sensation that arrowed straight between her legs.

"It doesn't matter."

Kayden swore, his fingers biting into the flesh of her ass.

"You might not be so dismissive when you discover the truth."

"Maybe not," she slowly agreed. "But…"

He frowned as she struggled to find the words to express the need aching deep inside her.

"But what?"

"I've spent twenty-two years being locked away and told it was for my own good," she confessed. "I don't won't to waste another second just because it might hurt me later."

His lips parted. He was going to continue to argue. She could feel it.

Framing his face in her hands, she tugged his head down to press her lips to his in a kiss of flagrant yearning.

Kayden went rigid and Bianca's heart began to sink. So much for her stumbling attempt at seduction.

Then, just as she was about to pull back in embarrassment, Kayden's arms lashed around her body and he hauled her off her feet so he could deepen the kiss with a stark urgency.

A combustion of heat blasted through her as his tongue skillfully parted her lips and dipped inside. She groaned. This was what she used to lay in her bed and fantasize about.

The hungry crush of his lips. The persistent stroke of his rough tongue. The arms that were wrapped around her as if he never intended to let her go.

Not about to allow him to have second thoughts, Bianca jumped up and circled her legs around his waist. They moaned in unison as her clit rubbed against his fully erect shaft.

Oh yeah. That's precisely what she needed.

The thought had barely formed when Kayden lifted his head,

regarding her flushed face with eyes that glowed with cognac fire.

"Bianca," he groaned, a feverish color staining his high cheekbones. "Dammit. You're killing me."

She nibbled up the curve of his neck, lapping at the droplets of water clinging to his bronzed skin.

"Do you want me to stop?"

He released a shuddering sigh. "Christ, no."

The scent of his musk thickened in the air, his cock pulsing with need.

"Good," she husked. "Then make love to me."

There was a charged silence as Kayden's savage need visibly battled with his conscience. Bianca held her breath, resisting the urge to beg.

Then, with a low growl he moved to the back of the shower, lowering her onto the slick marble bench. With a gentle tug he unlocked her legs from around his waist, although he kept them parted. She frowned, briefly confused until he knelt between them.

Their new position felt even more intimate, his gaze on level with hers, allowing her to watch the hunger in his cognac eyes as they ran a searing path over her breasts and down to her exposed feminine core. Arousal slammed through her, her hand lifting.

"Kayden," she breathed, tracing over his wide brow and down the slender line of his nose.

His eyes held the hunger of his animal as they returned to meet her steady gaze.

"My princess."

She flashed him a chiding smile. "Why do you keep calling me that?"

He captured her fingers that had been exploring his face, pressing them to his lips.

"That's how I think of you," he murmured. "An exquisite, rare beauty who has been hidden away. Just waiting for me to rescue her."

"My very own Prince Charming?"

"More like the Big Bad Wolf." His smile was wicked. "Or in this case, the big bad kitty."

Bianca's lips parted, but her words were stolen from her mouth as he leaned forward to kiss her with a stunning demand. Ah. Her arms wrapped around his shoulders, her head falling back as his lips stroked down the curve of her throat. She hissed out a soft breath as he nuzzled tender kisses over her wet face before rubbing their noses together in an oddly feline gesture of affection. Then, he was once again finding her mouth. This time his kiss was one of sheer possession.

Bianca's nails scored down the smooth skin of his back. She'd been prepared for his hungry onslaught, but his tender teasing was tugging at her vulnerable heart.

Wrapped in a fog of steam and the silence of the penthouse suite, it felt as if they were alone in the world. Bianca became lost in the sensual slide of Kayden's kiss and the light touch of his fingers as they roamed over her slick skin.

Bianca made a sound of restless need.

The water was turned off, so why did she feel as if she was drowning?

Kayden eased his kiss, allowing his lips to sweep over her upturned face. With care, he explored every line and curve, lingering on the erotic spot just below her ear, planting a path of kisses down the side of her neck.

"That feels so good," she breathed, shivering as his hands explored downward, finally cupping the taut fullness of her breasts.

"You fit perfectly in my palms," he muttered.

She barely listened to his soft words. She was too busy savoring the wicked bliss that was pulsing through her as his fingers lightly teased the puckered tips of her nipples.

He knew exactly how to touch her.

Pleasure shattered through her as he lowered his head and sucked one nipple between his lips.

A soft cry was wrenched from her lips as she tangled her fingers into the thick strands of his hair, arching toward him.

Lord, this was even better than her fantasies, she conceded, hissing with delight as his tongue and teeth made her shiver at the intensity of the sensations trembling through her body.

She wanted to beg him never, ever to stop. But at the same time she couldn't ignore the aching void between her legs that pleaded for attention.

"Kayden," she murmured, giving a restless tug on his hair.

"Patience, princess," he murmured.

Easy for him to say, she acknowledged with a flare of impatience. He hadn't been locked away in the middle of nowhere for years.

Bianca bit back her words as he lavished his attention on her other breast. Okay, she could learn a bit of patience. As long as those slender fingers continued to drift along the curve of her hip and down the length of her leg.

She allowed her head to drop back against the tiled wall of the shower as he licked her nipple with a growing insistence. At the same time, his fingers drifted up her inner thigh.

Ah, yes. He was headed in the right direction.

Then, amazingly he was there.

"Good God."

Her heart skittered, slamming against her ribs as his finger swept through her moist heat. It was like being jolted with a thousand watts of electricity. Her toes curled, her eyes squeezing shut.

With skillful ease, Kayden allowed his finger to linger on the tiny bundle of pleasure.

"Do you want more, princess?" Kayden rasped.

Was he kidding? She bit back a curse. She was fairly certain she was going to self-combust if she didn't get more.

Right now.

But even as the potent swell of her climax began to clench her muscles, she reached out to frame his face in her hands.

"I want to feel you, Kayden," she husked. "I want you inside me when I come."

The cognac eyes darkened with feral hunger, but he gave a slow shake of his head before he lowered his head to brush his lips over her breasts. Bianca's protest died on her lips as he glided his mouth slowly down her quivering stomach.

Clearly her kitty wanted to play.

As if to prove her right, Kayden gently tugged her legs farther apart. Then, leaning forward, he replaced his stroking finger with his tongue.

Holy crap.

Bianca moaned, her fingers knotting in his hair as he licked and nibbled and teased her with unmistakable expertise. Not that she minded his skill, she silently admitted, savoring the sensation of his tongue penetrating her tight channel before returning to concentrate on that small knot of nerves.

What female would protest at having a talented lover?

Her short pants of air echoed through the shower stall as the bliss spiraled higher and higher. Her back arched while her toes curled in anticipation.

Yes. It was glorious. Kayden was glorious.

As if sensing her climax was perilously close, Kayden secured his arms around her thighs and sucked her between his lips.

That was it. That was all that it took to make Bianca explode into a thousand pieces of pure ecstasy.

Swallowing her scream, she shivered with the violence of the tremors that continued to quake through her body as Kayden lapped at her clit.

Finally, Kayden gave her one last sweep of his tongue, then gently tugged her to her feet and wrapped her tightly in his arms.

"You taste like honey," he whispered into her hair, his lips grazing over her temple.

She clutched at his shoulders. Right now her knees weren't entirely reliable.

"Wow."

He chuckled. "That's the exact response I was hoping for."

"It was a perfect beginning," she breathed.

She felt his muscles clench beneath her hands, his head lifting to regard her with a wary gaze.

"Beginning?"

She allowed a sinful smile to curve her lips. She'd been a shy, timid creature her entire life.

Tonight she intended to be as bold and daring as she'd always wanted to be.

Holding his gaze, she skimmed one hand down his chest. A growl caught in his throat as she explored the rigid planes of his stomach.

"Bianca?"

"I still want to feel you inside of me."

His breath hissed between his clenched teeth, his hand reaching to grasp her wrist.

"In time."

"When?"

His eyes darkened. Pain? Need? A combination of both?

"I won't claim you until you know the full truth," he murmured.

Bianca grimly ignored the small stab of unease that pierced her heart.

She'd made her decision when she'd entered the shower that she wasn't going to worry about tomorrow. And if Kayden wanted to be stubborn, then she'd find some other way to play.

Plucking her wrist free of his grasp, she continued to explore down his body until she at last reached her goal.

"You told me that I was free to do what I want." She wrapped her fingers around his thick cock. "And this is what I want."

He sucked in a startled breath, but he wasn't stupid. A man understood it wasn't smart to wrestle with a woman when she was holding his pride and joy in her fingers.

"I'm not claiming you," he stubbornly growled. "Not until you know exactly what I've done."

"Fine." Already prepared for his stubborn refusal, Bianca pressed her lips to Kayden's chest, just above his racing heart. "I don't know exactly what you mean by claiming me, but if you won't have sex, then I intend to have my own fun."

"Fun?" he breathed as she planted a trail of kisses over his chest.

She could smell his rich musk drenching the air as she used her teeth to scrape against his skin. The tiny pain seemed to excite him. She smiled, moving her lips to his beaded nipple, giving it a sharp nip.

A low groan was wrenched from his throat, his fingers threading through her hair to hold her against him.

Accepting his silent plea for more, Bianca reveled in her sensual power. Kayden was the sort of sexy, intensely beautiful male who could attract the attention of any woman he wanted. But it was her touch that was making him shiver and groan.

Releasing the sensual side of herself that she'd always kept sternly repressed, she circled his nipple with the tip of her tongue even as her fingers traced the hard length of his erection. The skin was satin soft. And hot.

Holding his smoldering gaze, she slid her fingers down his cock, palming the heavy sack at the base. He growled, the veins of his neck visible as he reacted to her touch.

"Am I allowed to do this?" she husked.

"You don't play fair, princess." He was forced to halt and clear his throat, his face flushed with pleasure.

"Do you want me to stop?"

"Hell, no," he snarled.

"Ah."

With a sinful chuckle, she glided her fingers back to the tip of his cock, finding a tiny drop of moisture. She rubbed it lightly, circling the broad head before returning downward.

She repeated the caress over and over, keeping her touch light. Kayden hissed in pleasure, until her refusal to increase her slow, steady pace made him release his breath on an explosive sigh.

"Shit, Bianca, you're torturing me."

Although she was enjoying the power of having this glorious man at her mercy, Bianca wasn't a sadist. She wasn't going to make him beg for his release.

She lifted herself on tiptoes to press her lips softly to his mouth.

"Let's do it together."

With a choked groan of agreement, Kayden readily wrapped his hand over her fingers, pressing them hard against his cock. Then, together they stroked up and down the shaft, the heat from his body blasting through the air as his hips surged forward.

Bianca could feel his cock swelling and the musk of his cat threading through the steam. She squeezed her fingers tighter, pleased when Kayden gave a low growl of approval.

"Damn, princess, I can't wait," he ground out, his hand cupping the back of her head and urging her face toward his neck.

Instinct took over, and without knowing why, she sank her teeth into his firm flesh. She didn't break the skin, but the bite catapulted Kayden over the edge. With a raw groan of pleasure, he jackhammered their fingers up and down his cock, the warm spray of his seed covering their hands.

"I never knew how much fun a shower could be," Bianca murmured, kissing the side of his neck.

Chapter Six

Kayden didn't sleep.

Instead he rested on the vast bed with Bianca held tightly in his arms.

It was perfect, he decided, listening to the soft sounds of her breathing. The warmth of her body snuggled against him. The scent of honey lacing the air. The funny little noises she made when she was dreaming.

Or at least it would be perfect if there wasn't a tiny voice in the back of his mind whispering that he'd taken advantage of her.

After all, he'd told himself that he wasn't going to touch her after he'd watched her flee from the roof.

She was scared and disoriented, and utterly vulnerable. But when she'd walked naked into his shower, all his self-righteous intentions had been washed away.

It didn't matter that they hadn't actually had intercourse. As his grandmother would tell him, spraying perfume on a pig didn't make it a…hell, he couldn't remember what she said, but she would tell him that Bianca deserved better from him.

Silently promising to do everything in his power to make certain that she didn't regret sharing his shower, Kayden was distracted when his phone pinged with a text.

Careful not to disturb Bianca, he crawled from the bed and glanced at the message, his brows lifting in surprise.

Xavier was downstairs, demanding a meeting.

Pulling on his clothes, Kayden paused to brush a kiss over Bianca's tousled curls before he was heading out of the suite and down the elevator.

He halted at the lobby level and stepped out.

The hotel was muted. At five a.m., most of the guests had stumbled exhausted to their rooms, with only a handful of die-hard gamblers still drifting from table to table and the uniformed staff buzzing around in an effort to vacuum the carpets and polish the acres of marble.

He stepped into a small office behind the concierge desk, studying the large male with sharp features and buzzed hair who was leaning against the desk in the middle of the room.

"Good morning, Kayden," Xavier drawled, his large body covered by a black tee and jeans.

Kayden frowned. "How did you find me?"

Xavier shrugged. "I had all our vehicles hooked into my GPS system after the attack."

Kayden rolled his eyes. "Shit, I should have guessed," he said. Xavier had become compulsive in his need to keep track of pack members when they left the Wildlands. "What are you doing here?"

Xavier flicked a brow upward at Kayden's sharp tone. "I had an urge to see an Elvis impersonator. I heard Vegas was the place to come."

"Very funny," Kayden muttered.

Xavier shrugged. "Lex gave me a call."

Lex was a Pantera who was a silent co-owner of the hotel. He was the one who ensured there were a few rooms, including the penthouse suite, that were always available for his people.

He was also obviously a buttinsky, sticking his nose in where it didn't belong.

"Why?" he snapped.

Xavier shrugged. "He said that you were here with a woman."

See? A buttinsky.

"And why would that prompt a call?" Kayden demanded. "I can't imagine I'm the first male to share the penthouse suite with a female."

Xavier held his accusing gaze. "I asked him to keep an eye out for you," he admitted without apology.

"Why?"

"Because I was afraid your need for revenge would blind you to any potential dangers."

Kayden's annoyance abruptly evaporated. He wasn't angry with Xavier. Or even Lex.

He was pissed with himself.

"You have no idea," he muttered, ramming his fingers through his hair.

Xavier pushed away from the desk, instantly on full alert.

"What's going on, amigo?"

Kayden paused. It wasn't that he didn't trust Xavier. The male was as close as a brother to him. But his cat's possessive need to protect his mate made him reluctant to discuss her. With anyone.

"When I arrived at Ford's house I discovered he was in Florida," he forced himself to say, accepting that Xavier's arrival could actually help.

"Ford is the man who killed your parents?"

"Yes."

Xavier frowned in confusion. "You didn't follow him?"

Kayden shook his head, a humorless smile twisting his lips. "I had the brilliant idea to kidnap his daughter to force him to return."

Xavier sucked in a sharp breath. "You kidnapped an innocent woman?"

Kayden didn't blame his friend for studying him with an accusing expression. Pantera males were protectors, not predators when it came to females.

"It wasn't my finest moment," Kayden admitted. "Unfortunately, I wasn't thinking clearly."

"Kayden," Xavier began.

"Wait." Suddenly Kayden wanted it all out in the open. If he'd discovered nothing else, it was that secrets were as destructive as the most lethal weapon. "I'm not done."

Xavier arched a brow. "It gets worse?"

"Yes."

Xavier stepped toward him. "Tell me."

Kayden grimly met his companion's steady gaze. "After I brought her to Vegas I realized that she's Pantera."

The older male didn't bother to ask if Bianca had been born one of them or if she'd been injected with Pantera blood. As far as the Pantera were concerned, anyone with Pantera DNA was a part of their pack.

End of story.

"Where is she?" Xavier instead demanded, instantly kicking into protective mode.

"Upstairs sleeping."

"You didn't…" Xavier let the words trail away.

A growl of outrage rumbled in Kayden's chest at the obvious implication.

"I didn't hurt her," he snapped. "I couldn't. She's my mate."

"Mate?" Xavier closed his eyes, giving a shake of his head. "Christ. What a mess."

Kayden grimaced. Yep. It was a grade-*A*, first rate mess.

"I intend to fix it," he promised.

"How?" Xavier opened his eyes, his cat lurking in the depths of his blue eyes. "By killing her father? That's not really the sort of mating gift most women appreciate."

"I know." Kayden hunched his shoulders. "But I can't let him walk away. Not only because he killed my parents, but he's still running a laboratory that uses Pantera blood."

Without warning, Xavier reached into his front pocket to pull out a slender phone.

"I can take care of the laboratory," the male said, tapping in a quick message.

"Who are you texting?" Kayden demanded.

"Raphael." Xavier's lips twisted. "He insisted on coming. I think he was hoping he would have the opportunity to shed the blood of our enemies."

Ah. Relief jolted through Kayden. He was worried that the bastards working in the clinic would escape before he could get them rounded up.

Kayden pulled out his own phone, locating the GPS coordinates of the Cruise Clinic. He turned the screen so Xavier could see it.

"This is the location."

Xavier nodded, tapping in the numbers and sending them to Raphael. "Done."

"Fine." Kayden lowered his phone. "I still need to get my hands on Joshua Ford."

"What happens when you do?" Xavier asked, clearly accepting there was no point in trying to argue.

"I don't know for sure." Kayden shrugged. His emotions were too raw for him to be able to say for certain how he would react when he at last caught sight of the man who'd murdered his parents. "But I have to face him."

Xavier released a harsh sigh. "I get it, Kayden. I really do," he said.

"I'll go with you."

"No," Kayden swiftly refused. "I need someone to stay here with Bianca."

"I'll have Lex keep an eye on her," Xavier countered. "I intend to make sure that you aren't walking into a trap." He held up his phone. "Text me the coordinates of the meeting."

"You're a bossy bastard," Kayden muttered.

Xavier flashed a smile. "It's part of my charm."

"Says who?"

"My mate."

Kayden would have disputed the claim if he hadn't seen Xavier with his mate, Amalie. The two were goofy for one another. It was obvious in each soft glance and lingering touch.

They had the sort of connection that Kayden had always envied. The sort of connection that he hoped he could have with Bianca.

Lifting his phone, Kayden typed in the meeting place and sent it to his alpha.

"There," he muttered.

Xavier nodded. "What time is your meeting?"

Kayden glanced at his watch. Five thirty. "In less than an hour."

"I'll go scout the area," Xavier said, pocketing his phone.

Kayden reached out to lay his hand on his friend's shoulder. "Be careful no one sees you. I don't want to spook away my prey."

Heat sizzled through the air as Xavier glared at him in disbelief.

"I'd castrate you for that insult if I didn't know you're under a lot of stress," he growled, heading out of the office with long strides.

Kayden watched the male leave with a shake of his head.

A lot of stress? Ha. He was drowning under the strain.

The sooner he was done with Joshua Ford, the better.

Following Xavier out of the office, he moved to enter the manager's office, requesting Lex keep an eye on the penthouse suite in case Bianca woke up before he returned. Once assured that she wouldn't be able to leave the hotel without someone keeping a watch on her, Kayden headed to the back parking lot.

Lost in his thoughts, he slid into his truck, absently noting the rich scent of honey that seemed to cling to the air.

Bianca's musk had clearly imbedded in his skin, marking him as surely as the mating mark he intended to place on her. Just as soon as she agreed to spend the rest of eternity with him.

Starting the engine, Kayden pulled out of the lot and headed through the empty streets. He drove straight into the desert, heading toward Red Rock Canyon.

It was still dark when he arrived at the spot he'd demanded for the meeting, but dawn was beginning to brush the sky with hints of peach and deep lilac. He didn't need light, however, to catch sight of the expensive car that was parked near a flat area a few feet off the lone road that looped through the rough terrain.

Grabbing a handgun from the glove box, he stepped out of the truck, leaving the door open in case he needed a quick getaway. Then, allowing his senses to spread outward, he moved to stand in front of the hood of the truck.

He caught the scent of a coyote on the hunt for a scrambling rabbit and a lizard buried in the ground at his feet. But there were no humans that he could detect nearby.

"Get out of the car," he called out, hearing the buzz of an electric window being lowered a cautious inch.

"Where's my daughter?" a male voice demanded.

Kayden glared at the smoky windshield of the car. He'd bet his left nut that it was bulletproof.

"She's safe," he said.

"This meeting is over," the man said, his arrogant tone making Kayden's fingers tighten on the gun.

"Excuse me?"

"Until I can see for myself that you haven't harmed Bianca, I'm not speaking with you," the man informed him.

Kayden didn't bother with any melodramatic gestures like lifting his gun to point it at the car. Instead, he shrugged.

"Actually, I think you will," he said.

"No, I won't," the man snapped.

Kayden rolled his eyes. Trust a human to think because he was in a locked car with bulletproof glass that he was safe. Clearly he had no idea that Kayden could rip off the door with minimum effort.

"Then die," he said, taking a step forward.

The scent of fear abruptly spiced the air. "I have two sharp-shooters with their sights trained on you," Joshua bluffed. "One flash of my headlights and you're dead."

"You don't scare me," Kayden drawled.

He heard the rough sound of an indrawn breath. This meeting wasn't going as Joshua Ford had hoped.

Good.

"You're willing to have your brains splattered across the desert?" He once again tried to bluff.

On the point of rushing forward to yank open the door, Kayden froze as the scent of honey swirled on the breeze. Then, while his brain tried to process the knowledge that the sweetness couldn't just be lingering on his skin, there was the sound of movement as Bianca crawled out of the cargo container he kept in the back of his truck.

"Don't," she pleaded, jumping onto the sandy ground and moving to stand beside Kayden. "I'm here."

"Shit." A blast of fury exploded through Kayden. How had he been so stupid? Not even the fact he was distracted should have allowed him to dismiss her scent when he was getting into his truck. She must have suspected that he was planning to meet her father and snuck out of the room and hidden herself in the cargo container. Now she'd put herself in danger. "Bianca, get in the truck."

"No." She sent him a terrified glance. "I won't let my father hurt you."

His heart twisted. Christ. She'd risked herself because she was worried about him?

Reaching out, he intended to force her into the truck when there was the sound of a door opening and Joshua Ford stepped out of the car.

He was tall and lean, with hair that was perfectly combed and a gray suit that had no doubt been hand-tailored.

Kayden hated him on sight.

"Thank you, my dear," the man said, lifting a handgun and pointing it in their direction. "You've saved me a great deal of trouble."

Kayden was momentarily baffled. Not that the man had come armed, but that he would...

Realization hit a split second before Joshua pulled the trigger.

"No," he growled, darting in front of Bianca in time to take two shots to the center of his chest.

* * * *

Bianca had always wondered how she would react to an emergency. She'd wanted to believe that she would be cool and competent, just like her father.

Instead, she'd heard the gunshots and her mind had gone blank.

Thankfully, instinct kicked in as Kayden landed heavily against her. Wrapping her arms around his body, she used her surge of adrenaline to help drag him to the nearby truck, shoving him through the open door.

There was an echoing blast as her father took another shot, the bullet shattering the window in the door. Bianca gasped as the glass sliced through her cheek, but grimly pushing Kayden over, she climbed behind the steering wheel and shoved the gear into reverse. She slammed her foot on the gas, squealing the tires as she took off backward with a speed that had them bouncing over the dips and swells of the sandy ground.

Kayden groaned, and with a yank of the steering wheel that nearly tipped them over, Bianca turned the truck in a tight circle. Grinding the gearshift into drive, she punched the gas until they were traveling at a breakneck speed.

Dust streamed behind them, the tires bouncing as she headed toward the nearby hills. It was weird how flat the desert looked in pictures. In reality it was like driving over a massive washboard.

Glancing in the rearview mirror, she could see her father's car in the distance. It wasn't built with the same ability to dig through sand or climb over large rocks.

Thank God.

At last reaching the ridge of red sandstone hills, she darted between a natural archway and put the truck in park. It was still dark enough her father would have trouble knowing exactly where she'd gone. It seemed better to find a place to hide than to try and outrun him.

Turning in her seat, she watched as Kayden struggled to sit upright, his face pale.

She gasped, her eyes lowering to his shirt that had a hole ripped through the material and was coated in blood.

So much blood.

"Oh my God...Kayden."

Chapter Seven

She watched in horror as Kayden slid in and out of consciousness. Nearly twenty minutes passed before he finally struggled to sit upright, clearly still weak from the blood loss.

"Kayden," she breathed.

"It's okay, princess," he managed to rasp. "I'm already healing."

She reached out only to pull her hand back. She was terrified that she might hurt him.

"I'm sorry," she breathed.

His eyes glowed with a cognac fire in the darkness. "This isn't your fault, princess. None of this is your fault." He grimaced, giving a slow shake of his head. "I should have stayed at the hotel with you."

She bit her lower lip. When she'd heard him leaving the hotel room, she'd been certain he was planning to finish whatever it was that had brought him to her home. Determined to discover the truth, she'd slipped out of the hotel and hidden in the truck.

She'd never dreamed that she was about to witness the man she hoped to spend the rest of her life with being shot in the chest.

And by her own father.

"Why were you meeting with my father in the middle of the desert?" she abruptly demanded.

He hesitated. Why was he so reluctant to tell her the truth?

"For years I thought that my parents had died in an airplane crash. Recently I discovered proof that was a lie," he said, the words slow and slightly slurred.

She nodded, recalling his brief mention of his parents. "You said that humans killed them."

"Your father."

"I…" Her words failed as she realized that he was saying her father was somehow responsible for the death of his parents. "No," she breathed. "You have to be mistaken."

"It's true, Bianca." He reached to grab her hand. "They were taken captive by your father in San Francisco and held as prisoners in your father's clinic."

She shook her head, struggling to accept what he was telling her.

It seemed preposterous.

Her father could be cold and distant, and perhaps ruthless on occasion. But a killer?

Still, she'd watched with her own eyes as he'd deliberately shot Kayden, hadn't she?

"Why?" she breathed, shivering with belated shock. "He's a scientist."

"That's why," Kayden said in grim tones. "I told you, Benson Enterprises has been using my people as private lab rats for years. Your father needed Pantera and he kidnapped my parents." He was forced to pause, his hand clutched to his chest. "From what I could uncover, they were killed when they tried to escape the clinic."

She continued to shake her head. "I can't believe it."

He gave her fingers a squeeze. "I know it's hard, but it's the truth."

"So why…" Her words ended on a small gasp, her eyes widening as she was struck by a sudden realization. There was only one reason that Kayden would have taken her captive and then arranged to meet her father in such an isolated spot. "Oh, my God. You came here to kill my father."

He gave a slow dip of his head. "Yes."

Pain sliced through her. Now she understood why he'd been so reluctant to confess the truth.

"Did you intend to kill me too?"

"No." Horrified shock rippled over his face that was tight with pain. "I would never hurt you."

"You didn't think shooting my father was going to hurt me?" she demanded.

"During my drive here I'd already decided that I would capture him instead," he told her, a raw edge of regret in his voice. "I can't let him walk free, princess. Not when he's a danger to the Pantera. But I wasn't going to put a bullet through his heart as I'd originally planned."

She believed him.

Not just because she wanted to, but because there was something inside her that was convinced she would know if he was lying.

"Why did you change your mind?"

He leaned toward her, his eyes darkening as his cat prowled close to the surface.

He didn't hesitate. "Because your happiness is more important than my revenge."

The air was knocked from her lungs. All her life she felt as if she was a burden, more of a patient than a daughter.

Never once had she ever had anyone consider her happiness.

"Oh, Kayden," she breathed, leaning forward to press a light kiss on his cheek. "And instead my father tried to kill you," she said.

"Not me," he said in low tones. "You."

She jerked back, her eyes widening in confusion. She'd assumed that her father had sought to kill Kayden because he was trying to rescue her.

Now her brain struggled to absorb his words.

"What?"

"He wasn't trying to shoot me," he insisted, his expression bleak. "He was aiming at you."

"He's quite right, my dear," a male voice drawled before her father was stepping from the shadows. "I was aiming at you."

"Father," she hissed, stiffening as she felt Kayden reach out to give her leg a warning squeeze.

She wasn't exactly sure how her father had managed to find them. Perhaps he'd followed their tracks that had no doubt been left in the soft dirt. And right now it didn't matter. Her only concern was to keep the older man talking until Kayden could finish healing. Licking her dry lips, she forced herself not to flinch as he stood next to the window he'd so recently shot out.

"Why would you want to hurt me?" she demanded in a voice that shook with a combination of fear and fury. "I'm your daughter."

He shook his head, his expression unreadable. "Actually, you're not."

"I'm not?" Bianca stared at Joshua Ford, feeling as if she was looking at a stranger.

And in truth, she was.

It was obvious that her entire life had been a lie.

He shook his head. "My daughter died of cancer when she was just a baby."

His daughter? She gave a faint shake of her head. "I don't understand." The understatement of the century.

"It was simple," he drawled, his gaze flicking toward Kayden, who was leaning heavily against her shoulder, as if still weak from his injuries. She was praying that he was merely faking. If her father…no. If Joshua Ford had followed them, it wasn't to tell her that he'd been lying to her for years. "My daughter, Bianca, was diagnosed not long after her birth. My wife wanted to use traditional treatments, but I'd heard of Benson Enterprises and the amazing research they were doing. I took Bianca and we traveled to the Cruise Clinic where I was given a full, private lab for my research to work on a cure."

Any sympathy for his confession that his young daughter was sick was destroyed by his cold lack of emotion. He might as well have been speaking about a stranger, not his precious baby.

"A cure that used Pantera blood?" she demanded, recalling Kayden's insistence that Joshua had kidnapped his parents.

"Of course." Joshua shrugged, not seeming to hear Kayden's low growl. Or to notice the anger that sizzled through the air. It was a stark reminder that he was human, while she was…different. "I gathered a half dozen of the animals, including you and your mother."

"My mother?" Her breath felt as if it was being squeezed from her lungs. "She was Pantera?"

Another shrug. "Yes."

"I don't remember her," she choked out. There'd always been a hole in her heart at the lack of a mother's love.

He waved a dismissive hand. "You were an infant."

A faint hope flared through her. "Where is she?" she demanded.

"Dead." he said, his voice stripped of emotion. Or more likely, Joshua Ford didn't possess emotions. He was a cold-hearted snake who used people like they were no more than pieces on a chessboard. "She was trying to protect you from becoming a part of my experiments and my guards became a little…overenthusiastic."

A sound of pain was wrenched from her throat, but even as her hand reached toward the handgun that Kayden had hidden between them, she felt Kayden give her leg another squeeze.

A silent warning.

He clearly had a plan. Which meant she couldn't shoot Joshua in the face.

"You bastard," she choked out. "Why pretend I was your daughter?"

"Within a year it became obvious that I wasn't going to be capable of curing my daughter, but I still had the opportunity to achieve my career goals."

Her lips curled in disgust. "Your career goals?"

A hint of smug satisfaction settled on the lean face. "I've always been ambitious."

Well, at least one part of him hadn't been a lie. His ego was just as bloated and pretentious as she'd suspected, even when she was young.

"What does that have to do with me?"

"I couldn't admit that the cure for my daughter had been a failure," he said, a hint of impatience in his voice, as if he couldn't believe she would even have to ask. "So instead, I got a new daughter."

Her stomach clenched with revulsion. How had she lived with this man for so long and not realized he was a complete whack job?

"You're sick," she ground out. "Truly sick."

Annoyance flared through his eyes. Clearly he didn't like having his lack of sanity pointed out.

"I've always been destined for greatness. I just needed the chance to prove it," he snapped, a dark color crawling beneath his skin. "You were my ticket to receiving unlimited funding for the clinic."

She narrowed her eyes. "So if you need me, why would you shoot at me?"

"My benefactor has suddenly decided it's time to meet you. I can't allow them to discover that you're a full-blooded Pantera." He took a step back, lifting his arm to reveal the gun clutched in his hand. "I am sorry, my dear. I have become…" He paused, searching for the proper word. "Very fond of you."

"Fond?" she breathed. Loathing mixed with her stark terror.

Then, she was distracted as there was a brief flash of light just behind Joshua. Without warning, Kayden grabbed her by the back of her neck and jerked down.

She heard the echo of a gunshot. Joshua gave a grunt and fell against the truck before he crumpled to the ground.

Bianca pressed her face into Kayden's neck, concentrating on the steady sound of his heartbeat as the scent of Joshua Ford's blood filled the air.

Chapter Eight

Less than ten minutes later, Kayden was crawling into the back of Xavier's Jeep and clutching Bianca tightly in his arms.

He'd tried to keep her from seeing Joshua Ford stretched dead on bloody sand as he'd waited for his friend to arrive. She'd endured enough shocks as she'd been forced to listen to Ford reveal she was nothing more than a means to climb the corporate ladder. Not to mention the fact that her mother had been murdered by the man who'd pretended to be her father.

Christ.

He'd wanted to put a bullet through the man, but he'd already caught sight of Xavier climbing onto a nearby rock to get the best angle to kill him without putting Bianca in danger. So he'd forced himself to wait.

Settling back in the seat, he sent Xavier a glare as the older male glanced into the rearview mirror.

"Took you long enough.

Xavier grimaced as he put the Jeep into gear and headed in a direct line for the road.

"Sorry. I wasn't expecting your female to take off like a bat out of hell. It took a few minutes to get back to my vehicle and by then you'd disappeared. I decided to follow Joshua to make sure he didn't escape."

"My female." Kayden pressed his lips to the top of Bianca's head, breathing in her honey scent. "I like the sound of that."

Bianca lifted her hand to lightly touch his chest. His wound had nearly healed. Within an hour there would be nothing to indicate he'd been shot.

"Me too," she murmured.

His arms tightened around her shivering body. Shock was just setting in.

"I'm sorry about your father," he murmured softly.

She gave a sharp shake of her head. "Joshua was never my father. In fact, I don't know who was my biological father, but someday I intend to find out."

"True, he wasn't your father. Still—"

His words were cut off as Bianca lifted her fingers and pressed them against his lips.

"No," she said in a firm tone. "I want the past to stay in the past. At least for now."

He rubbed his cheek against hers in a purely feline gesture. Eventually they would both have to confront what Joshua Ford had done to them and work through the pain. But for now, he just wanted to celebrate having this kind, gentle, exquisitely beautiful female in his arms.

"I couldn't agree more," he murmured. "All I want is to concentrate on my mate."

Xavier cleared his throat. "Are you ready to go home?"

Kayden slowly lifted his head, gazing down at Bianca's pale face. As anxious as he was to take her to the Wildlands and introduce her to her new pack, he had a more pressing desire at the moment.

"Actually, I want to go back to Vegas," he told his friend.

"Vegas?" Xavier demanded in surprise.

"Yeah." He lips curved in a sensuous smile as he watched Bianca's cheeks flush with anticipation. "Bianca and I have some unfinished business that includes complete privacy and a large shower."

Xavier chuckled, stepping on the gas. "You got it."

Leaning down, Kayden brushed a kiss over Bianca's willing lips.

"Viva, Las Vegas."

* * * *

Bianca arched against Kayden's hard muscles anticipation licking through her body with flames of pleasure.

They were already naked and lying in the bed they'd shared the night before after spending an hour in the shower. Kayden had kissed and caressed her until she was at the point of screaming with the need to ease the insistent desire he'd stroked to a fever pitch.

He'd adamantly refused to listen to her pleas, insisting that they enjoy their first time together in the comfort of a bed.

Now she studied his beautiful face. His lean features had softened, his eyes glowing with the heat of his cat.

"Are you having second thoughts?" she asked, trying to keep her voice teasing. Inside, she truly worried that he might have decided that she wasn't the female he wanted to share his life with.

He frowned, then without warning, he was rolling her onto her back so he could perch on top of her. She shivered, savoring the feel of his solid weight pressing her deep into the mattress. Instinctively her legs parted, allowing him to settle between her thighs, the tip of his cock pressed against her clit.

"I'm a Pantera," he said on a growl. "Once we choose our mates, there are never any second thoughts. Our love and devotion is unwavering. And eternal."

"Mate." The word echoed through her, easing the restlessness that twisted her stomach into knots.

He studied her with a hunter's gaze, the heat of his body feeling as if it was scalding her sensitive skin.

"Does that work for you?"

She shuddered, her hands reaching up to frame his face. "Oh, it works," she assured him in soft tones. "An eternity with you is exactly what I want."

A wicked smile curved his lips. "What else do you want?"

She didn't hesitate. "You. I want you."

"Music to my ears," he rasped, lowering his head to capture her lips in a kiss of sheer possession.

Bianca released a soft moan, heart racing as she allowed her fingers to tangle in the short strands of his hair. He tasted of mint and heat and raw male power. Her head spun, the desire he'd already stirred to life thundering through her as his tongue dipped between her lips.

"Kayden, please," she pleaded.

"Yes," he muttered, reaching down to guide his straining erection to the entrance of her body. "Hold on, princess."

Holding her wide gaze, he penetrated her damp channel.

Bianca released a soft breath as he pressed ever deeper. There was a burning sensation as he invaded her.

He seemed excessively large. Were all men this big? His hardness seemed to be stretching her to the limit. Then he was finally buried deep inside her.

Now her groan was one of fierce approval. Oh, yeah. This was want she'd wanted. It was everything that she'd dreamed of.

Spreading her knees, she silently encouraged him to continue. She might not know a damned thing about making love, but she sensed that Kayden was a master.

Relishing his slow, steady pace, Bianca spread her hands over his chest, her eyes widening as he held up one hand and deliberately allowed his claws to pierce the tips of his fingers. Her breath caught as he held her gaze and with one slashing motion, he'd sliced his claws through the tender skin of her hip.

It should have hurt, but instead she felt nothing but a burst of tingling magic that exploded through her. A power at the very center of her being roared to life, stretching toward Kayden even as his roar of satisfaction shook the air.

Her inner cat?

Perhaps.

Kayden wrapped his arms around her, burying his face in the curve of her neck. Then, pumping into her at a furious pace, his fingers stroked over the marking on her hip at the same time he catapulted her into a shattering climax.

Bianca quivered in ecstasy, convulsing around him as he gave one more thrust and cried out with the violent pleasure of his own orgasm.

"Mine," she called out.

"Mine," he panted. "For all eternity."

Simon

Chapter One

"Shift back," Parish growled as he stood at the cabin door, arms crossed over his bare chest. "I've had about enough of this bullshit, Tryst."

Behind the screen, the massive midnight-black cat grinned up at him.

Damn female. Pain in his ass.

"This isn't a friend making a request, Tryst," he continued with barely disguised irritation. "This is your commander."

The cat raised one eyebrow. Which, frankly, would seem like an impossible feat for a puma—but this puma wasn't like any other.

Parish exhaled heavily.

"I'll jump back into my cat, boss," Lian said, holding ground right beside him. "Discuss things with her. Use a little fangs and claws. You know, the language she understands."

Parish turned his head and uttered tersely, "Get serious. You know her. Have since you were cubs." He gave the male a pointed look. "You know what she's capable of. You try and cross this threshold, you'll get your ass handed to you."

Lian's lip curled. "Bullshit. She's barely out of cubhood. A female. And half my size—"

With a sudden crash, the black puma shot forward and attacked the screen, cutting off the male's words and sending him, and Parish too, back a good two feet. Both males cursed as, with a snarl of satisfaction, the puma dropped to all fours once again.

"All show, no bite," Lian baited, though remained where he was.

"Shut it," Parish said to the male, then approached the door once again. "Okay, Tryst, enough of the games. This isn't just any order. And I'm not the only one giving it. You remember Raphael, don't you? Our leader?"

Parish waited for the hiss or the snarl that normally accompanied a reminder of authority. But this time, the cat was silent. Even sat down on her haunches. Pale blue eyes wary, she glared up at him, as if to say, *Yes, asshole, I know him.*

"This is dire," Parish continued. "The species—your Pantera—need you."

Her nostrils flared, as if she was trying to scent his sincerity. And if anyone could do it, it would be her. She was a strange thing. Talented, brave, and ruthless...but strange.

"No one has your capture and retrieving skills, female. With fur or without." He leaned against the doorjamb and inhaled sharply. "I know you're not comfortable doing the without thing, but we need this male."

Pumas didn't have eyebrows, but this one did. Maybe it was because she practically lived in her cat 24/7 and her human traits had fused somehow with the animal ones. Whatever the reason, she raised that brow high and in question.

"I don't know why they want him," Parish told her. He pulled a piece of paper from his back pocket and thrust it flat against the screen door. It was barely a paragraph. All they had on the rogue Diplomat. "Raphael won't disclose it to me. But he made it very clear that this is vital—life and death kinda thing—and to get my best on it."

Behind him, Lian snorted. "Best," he grumbled. "Please. I'm right here, boss."

Parish didn't have a chance to respond. To tell the male to pipe down or they were going to lose Tryst and her skills. The front door of the cabin burst open with a sharp creaking sound and the puma leapt out. With barely a sound, she snatched the paper from Parish's hand with her teeth, then, as both males watched—mouths open—she leapt from the porch steps and took off into the misty morning bayou.

Chapter Two

Didn't they get it? No one fucking touched his hair but him. Not because he was a vain prick with an attitude problem, but because if they did, if they got too close, they'd see the tats on his scalp. The marks he'd been given in hopes he could be tracked. Hadn't worked, of course. But the tats remained.

As a reminder not to get that close to being caught ever again.

"Simon." The photographer's assistant stuck her head into the room. The twenty-something female gave him a bright white smile, her gray eyes eager. "They're ready for you."

"Thank you…" he said with a question mark to his tone.

"Becca," she supplied.

"Right."

Her smile faltered and her eyes flickered to the floor. She was disappointed he hadn't remembered her name. He wished he could tell her it wasn't anything personal. It wasn't arrogance or douchebaggery either. He'd seen her once on the way in, but hadn't worked with her before. In fact, he never worked with the same photog more than once, so he rarely remembered anyone's name. Such was his life. And his rules of order. Never stay in one place long enough to develop relationships. Business or otherwise. Trust no one. Rely on no one. He worked only to stay flush, jobs coming through his private Instagram account only. And before he agreed, all parties and locations were checked out thoroughly. Granted, he'd fucked up a time or two. Drew some unwanted fur his way. But it had been a clear thirteen months since those fangs had attempted to come 'round. Maybe his past had finally gotten the message.

"Can I get you something to drink?" Becca asked, following closely behind as he left the dressing room and headed for the set.

"No, thanks, darlin'. I'm good."

The shoot was for Red Dog men's fragrance. Something he'd never smelled or worn in his life. Fragrance, even scented soap, brought out his musk, and he couldn't have that. The fact that he didn't wear what he was selling didn't seem to bother the company heads, though. Hell, they were giving him the billboard in Times Square. It was his biggest score yet, and despite the exposure issue—which would drive him underground for a year or so—he should be happy as a pig in shit. After all, the payday would fill his bank account to the brim, not to mention buy him that little house in Athens he had his eye on—the one that could serve as his "underground." But happiness was not something he considered possible. Inside the Wildlands or living among the humans. Once stolen and ravaged, an emotion like that, so precious, so rare, was gone forever.

"All right, Simon?" the photographer called over to him.

Simon assessed the set. Craggy brick wall, gray concrete floors, plush red velvet couch. He headed for the red velvet and dropped to his knees before it. Instantly, the photographer started clicking away. He moved lithely through poses: arms stretched out wide, head falling back, cheek resting on the cushion, eyes eating up the lens...

Strange job, modeling. But it spoke, and encouraged, every facet of the...Goddess, could he even think the words anymore?

The Pantera within him.

Yes, he supposed he could think of it.

He grinned. His Pantera nature rose to the surface with every fierce look he threw at the camera.

"Not sure I'm feeling the tux, Simon," the photographer called out. "What about you?"

Simon turned to see the man staring into his camera, assessing, as he moved through the shots.

"Fragrance goes on the skin," Simon replied, removing his jacket and tossing it aside.

Ever so slowly he pulled off his tie, then started ripping his shirt away from his body. As buttons flew and fabric shredded, the photographer quickly jumped in and started snapping, calling out, "Oh, hell yeah. Loving this. Eyes on the lens and walk to me. Slowly. Tear me apart while you're tearing the shirt."

Mouth slightly open, teeth bared, Simon did as he was commanded, embodying what he'd left behind. Or who… The Pantera male. The beast man…without the beast…

"Perfect," the photog said. "I'm following your lead."

Tossing the shirt off set, Simon turned and stalked toward the red velvet couch. Slipping the belt from the pants at his waist, he sat down, legs spread wide, grabbed the *New York Times* off the coffee table and started to read.

"Too much?" he uttered, keeping his face covered but his chest exposed.

No answer. Just the familiar clicking sound of the camera's shutter as the photog moved in closer.

* * * *

A *model?*

Were they fucking kidding her with this?

Was this a…joke?

Sending their best tracker…forcing her out of her fur—for this?!?

Poised, ready, disgusted, Tryst sneered from her spot beside a support beam in the shadows of the warehouse as she stared at the Pantera male sitting on the red couch. No. He wasn't worthy of that name. The near-human male?

Yes. Perfect.

He had tossed the newspaper he'd been fake-reading onto the floor and was now staring straight into the camera. Ravenous. Long legs spread wide, tan chest hard with muscle, overly handsome facial features taut and fierce and lightly stubbled. With short black hair tousled like…well, like he'd just had a good fuck. She supposed he was something to behold. No doubt he was over six four and could bench press a Ducati too, like most Pantera males…

A flash of unwanted heat flickered through Tryst with both that look and his predatory body language, but she shoved it away. Hell no. No spark of attraction for the nearly-human male model. *Yuck! Disgusting.* Allowing herself to feel such things made her unworthy of her fur. Even if, for one second, she'd sworn she'd seen it. The puma inside him. The one she hadn't believed existed when she'd stepped into this laughably guarded warehouse five minutes ago. Her eyes narrowed on the male. But it was there. Inside him. Down deep, controlled by something… His will, perhaps? Brought out whenever he stared into the camera. Making the photographer nearly explode with hunger in his designer denim.

Asshole. Traitor. *Simon: the male model.* He was using the Pantera inside him, what he once was, to entice a human audience. Sell a human scent. He disgusted her, repelled her. In fact, she had a mind, and a will, to charge in, make a meal of anyone who got in her face, grab that sexy sellout by the waist of his fancy tuxedo pants and be on her way. Back to real life. To the bayou. But the scent of agitated human female coming up behind her captured her nostrils and drew her attention away.

"Are you serious with that?" the woman whispered.

Tryst turned to glare at the young, college-aged female who'd found her in the shadows. "Is there a problem?" she asked the harmless gnat.

The severe tone in her voice caught the girl by surprise and she inhaled sharply. "Look," she stumbled with a shaky sort of smile. "His contract states bubbled water only. Just trying to save your butt. You know?"

For a brief second, Tryst had no clue what the gnat was talking about. Bubbles? Wasn't that something human children played with? Or bathed in? Then she spied the table to her right. Laid out on a blue cloth were breads, fruit, sweets and several bottles of sweating water. Her gaze returned to the girl. Clearly, she believed Tryst to be some kind of model's servant.

The fangs hidden inside her gums vibrated.

Gnats loved blood, didn't they? Well, so did Pantera.

This one, anyway.

"Models are weird that way," the girl explained with a quiet laugh. "Superstitious or something. I don't know this guy personally or anything"—she pointed at the faux-Pantera—"but I'm willing to bet he'll freak out if he doesn't have his bubbles."

Tryst sniffed. "Will he now?" Oh, Parish was going to pay for this. He'd selected her for a mission of ridiculousness. Truly, her puma had always had it in for him. Ever since he'd made it swim the bayou to save one of the new recruits.

She fucking hated water.

"You don't want to get fired, do you?" the girl asked.

"Oh, Goddess forbid," Tryst said dramatically, and no doubt sarcastically. She turned away from the girl and focused back on the male, who no doubt used to run and capture prey, leap from trees, growl at his enemies—know who the fuck he was.

The male who now wanted BUBBLE WATER.

"Gorgeous, isn't he?" the gnat said, lust threading her tone.

Yuck.

"Not my type," Tryst muttered.

There was a snort of amusement behind her. "Oh, come on. Hot, rich male models are everyone's type, honey."

Call me that again and I will disembowel you. "I play for a different team."

The girl inhaled sharply. "Oh, right. Gotcha. Cool."

Tryst's lips twitched with humor as she watched Simon, the model, undo the top button of his tux pants and splay them just enough to expose a sprinkling of black hair at his taut groin. Once again, the unsettling feeling came over her, and once again she forced it away. The team she played for wasn't the one this male had joined. Her team was male all right, but he was dangerous, determined, covered in fur and could give two shits about money, cameras, or bubbles in his water.

What did Raph want with this traitor, she wondered, as against her will her mouth watered. He was clearly one of them now. A human. Weak. What could he possibly have that the Pantera needed so badly—so desperately? And why had she been led to believe that finding and capturing him would be a nearly impossible task? Locating him had been a breeze. Getting on set? A day at the shore.

Maybe he knew someone? Was connected?

Shit, maybe he was bait.

He was perched on the back of the couch now, like a hawk, buttoned up at the waist again and holding a pair of thick black glasses between his fingers. As he slid them on, his gaze flickered in her direction and held. A sharp pain erupted inside her chest and heat circled her belly. She inhaled deeply and stepped back a foot, trying to escape the sensations running rampant within her. What the hell was that? The way he was posed? The glasses? Goddess, maybe she had an undiscovered turn-on for them—after all, none of the Pantera wore them, so she wouldn't really know. Whatever it was, it had made her insides go crazy—it had made her gasp.

And she didn't gasp.

Ever.

Not even when she mated from time to time with one of the males she deemed worthy enough for a casual night…or morning…of fun.

Eyes three shades darker than her own pale blue, and encircled by masculine black frames, narrowed on her. She told her body, her insides, to stand the hell down or else. She had a job to do. But across the room, he kept staring. Hard. Did he know who she was? What she was?

Someone elbowed her in the back, and she whirled around and snapped, "What?"

It was the girl. Again. She drew back, eyes wide, and swallowed. "I'm just saying...well, go." She pointed past Tryst. "Give it to him. And good luck with holding on to your job. I told you he wanted bubbles."

Oh, shit. The water. The gnat seriously thought she was an assistant. Of course, why else would she be on set, right? She inhaled sharply and planned her movement. Wouldn't do to draw attention to herself. The title of assistant worked for her...though if the male model scented her...

Hmmm...she couldn't remove him from the set without questions or cops being called. Too open. She needed to draw him out, then strike when he was in his dressing room. She cursed herself for not waiting in there for him to begin with. But she'd wanted to check him out. Make sure he was the one she sought. See what kind of threat he truly was—

"Girl, forget getting fired, you'll never work in fashion again if you don't move," the gnat uttered. "Oh, great. Now the photographer is looking over here. I'd do it myself but I'm not getting canned for your mistake."

"Relax, honey," Tryst said, grabbing a couple bottles from the food table and breaking free from the shadow. She tossed one to the photographer as she moved past him. "Nice save, captain," she called out when he caught it easily, his eyes wide and confused.

She didn't wait for a response, just continued on her way. Her prey was ahead and watching her every move. Left, right, left right. He slipped off the red velvet couch just as she came to stand before it. His gaze ran the length of her and when it returned to her eyes, they were glistening. She grinned. She wasn't wearing anything that would cause a male to gawk. Tight black jeans, black tank, black combat boots, her mass of red hair pulled into a topknot high on her head. But attraction or sex or hunger wasn't what glistened in his eyes—or what hardened his...jaw.

"Who are you?" he demanded, low and dangerous, his nostrils flaring as he breathed her in.

"Your assistant, hot stuff." Every word dripped with disgust and sarcasm. "Or should I call you, Mr....I'm sorry, do you even have a last name? Is that a model thing?"

A sound rumbled in his throat. It was deadly and went inside her chest and vibrated. Hard. *Oh, my.* So maybe he was Pantera after all. Albeit a shadow of one.

He crossed his arms over his broad, lean-muscled chest and laughed softly. "Getting desperate, is he?"

"The photographer? Probably." She smiled but knew the show of teeth didn't reach her eyes. "I think you gave him what he wanted, though."

The male sobered. "Raphael," he returned very slowly, enunciating each syllable of the name so that at the end, his tongue flicked his teeth.

Goddess be damned. That tongue. She couldn't take her eyes from it. Her faux smile faltered as what felt like hot ash sizzled deep in her belly. She was really starting to hate this male.

"He sent you here to bring me back, isn't that right?" he asked, his eyes crashing into hers and demanding the truth. "To the Wildlands? Home?"

"Back to the *bayou*, is what you mean to say," she clarified with venom that stemmed from not only her growing dislike of this male, but the strange shock of heat he seemed to create that was continuously coursing through her blood. "The Wildlands isn't your home. More like a page in some fashion rag. But yeah," she added on a sigh. "He wants you back." She shoved the water at him. "Finish up here, pretty boy. Then go take off your makeup and put on something that won't shame you or me." She turned around and called over her shoulder, "Oh yeah—and sorry, not sorry, about the lack of bubbles."

Chapter Three

He hadn't been away from the bayou long enough to believe that the tall, staggeringly gorgeous female standing in the middle of his dressing room was an unskilled, newbie Hunter. He knew what Raphael sent his way. They got more aggressive and hyper-brilliant every time. So this one had to be something not to underestimate. Unless the big boss believed Simon would cave to the needs of a hard dick. Because truly, that shit could be a powerful motivator. And the female before him with her fists full of red hair, body of a Venus, eyes the color of the Athens sky, and a full mouth with a razor-sharp tongue had caused both. Forget the boney, blank-eyed models he worked with. This female was truly something significant. Something to lust after.

He shoved down his zipper. "You might want to turn away, female."

As predicted, she sneered. "Why's that?"

"I need to change my clothes."

"And?"

"Don't wear underwear."

She sniffed with forced boredom. "Please."

"Just being a gentleman, darlin'."

"I ate one of those for breakfast on my way over here." She grinned. "Male."

Savage heat flickered in Simon's chest at her words. Or maybe it was *that* word. He hadn't been called it in a long time, and for a second, he thought it might have awakened...

No. Impossible.

The Pantera inside of him was dead. And very much forgotten.

He growled to himself as he kicked off his shoes.

"You know what I want," she said smoothly. "You, coming with me, all nice and quiet—"

"I never come quiet, female." He stared at her, his brow lifted as he yanked off his pants and tossed them over a chair.

Her jaw tightened and a stain of heat bloomed on her cheeks. "Back to the Wildlands where you belong," she added pointedly. Her eyes narrowed on him but never dropped below his neck. "Or where Raph seems to think you belong."

"Raphael needs to leave well enough alone." Naked now, he stalked over to the clothing rack and grabbed a pair of jeans and T-shirt.

"Raphael is your leader," she said in a vicious tone. "Whether you live inside the Wildlands or out. Pretend if you want, but you're not human. You're Pantera."

When he headed back her way, her gaze skimmed over him. Assessing. Every inch.

"Goddess only knows why he wants you." Her gaze dropped and she stared mockingly at his cock, which was halfway hard now. "Hmmm…maybe I'm mistaken. Maybe you're not Pantera after all."

With a flash of speed, he was on her, had her momentarily off her feet, then pressed back against the dressing room door. "Ever think it's about you, not about me?"

"No."

He grinned, his cock no longer at half-mast but fully erect. Oh, yes, it was definitely about her. "You think you're the first one they sent to bring me back, female? You think they haven't tried this nearly every other month for the past five years?"

By the look on her face, she didn't know. Of course they hadn't told her. And she'd not demanded it. Just had gone blindly into her mission. No questions asked. The Pantera. Sense of duty was bullshit.

He leaned in and sniffed her neck—oh, *just a taste*—then lifted his head and whispered in her ear, "You've wasted your time coming here."

Her growl carried a thread of sexual energy.

His tongue lapped at her lobe. "Go home, kitten."

She grabbed him suddenly, forearms cinching his waist, and somehow managed to turn him around. *Goddess!* In seconds, it was he who was pressed back against the door.

His arms pinned over his head.

Oh, fuck, yes. He laughed softly, his eyes locked with hers. This was his kind of female. If only she wasn't a pain in the ass Hunter who had vowed to capture and return him to his personal hell. "Just went from semi to block of wood, kitten," he uttered, his voice threaded with needed. "Yank 'em back even farther, will you. Pain is what I live for."

It wasn't the response she was expecting and her eyes flickered with unease. "What is wrong with you?"

Her mouth was calling to him. "Nothing that can't be cured living away from the Wildlands."

"Sorry. Not possible."

Goddess, he wanted to grab her ass and lift her up, make her straddle him. Find some relief. It wouldn't be difficult. She was strong but not nearly strong enough to contain him. "You gonna walk me out of here like this?"

"Why not?"

"Oh, I don't know. Besides the bareass naked issue, a lot of photographers out there. NYPD will be called. Attention will be drawn." He lifted his chin a fraction. Better to smell her with. "Did they teach you nothing in Hunter school? When you go outside the Wildlands, you don't draw attention to yourself and your kind."

With a curse, she pushed away from him, releasing his wrists. "Get dressed."

"It'd go faster if you helped."

She dropped into a chair and snorted. "No interest in touching you."

"You're just going to leave me like this?"

"I'm sure it's not the first time."

He laughed and pushed away from the door. She was feisty. A true cat. Spitting one moment, purring the next. It was disappointing that he'd never see her again after today. But such was life. Well, his life.

He pulled on his shirt then grabbed his jeans. "Can I ask you something?"

"What?" she practically snarled.

"Why do you love it? The Wildlands?" He zipped up and put on his shoes. "Don't you feel caged there? Like an…animal?"

"I love being an animal. I wish I had fur on my back right now."

"That's right," he recalled. "No shifting outside the magic of the Wildlands… So...are you in your cat more often than you're like this?" He walked toward her, his gaze flickering past her for a brief second.

"If I could be in my cat 24/7, I would."

"Interesting."

She stood up. "Can we go now." It wasn't a question, and his answer wasn't a verbal one.

He reached behind her, yanked the chair forward, which made her falter, her butt landing on the cushion once again. He leaned in close, his eyes locked with hers, his face just an inch away. "Cab waiting outside? Or is it a limo? Maybe a horse-drawn carriage? I'm used to grand gestures."

For a few brief seconds—which was all he needed—the female seemed to consider this. Then her lips twitched and her eyes took on a mocking look. She was damn good at those looks. Made his knees buckle. Almost.

"I'm thinking I'll just throw you over my shoulder, caveman style." She batted her eyelashes. "Or cavewoman."

He groaned. This sucked. "Goddess, you don't know how good that sounds." He stood up, exhaling with disappointment. "Another time. I hope."

She sniffed and rolled her eyes, then started to rise. When she realized she was tied to the chair, her gaze blasted his and she bared her teeth.

"You piece of rotting shit," she snarled.

He grabbed his bag. "I know you don't mean that, kitten."

Like the wildcat she was, she started fighting, growling and straining hard against the nearly invisible threads that bound her. But to no avail. She wasn't going anywhere. It was amazing stuff. Found and purchased in a small town just outside Frankfurt, Germany.

"It only gets tighter when you struggle," he informed her. "Listen, if it's any consolation, I've never wanted to…" He gave her a wicked, regretful smile.

"Fuck you," she spat at him.

"Yes, that exactly. I've never wanted that with any of the other Pantera Raph has sent my way. You're quite something." He reached for his coat. "Tell your leader that my life is my own. And next time he thinks to send someone to fetch me, let him know I may not be sending them back alive."

He turned and walked out the door, sure to lock it behind himself.

* * * *

Not possible.

Not. Fucking. Possible.

Had she just basically allowed that traitor to contain her? Had she—a Hunter, a self-described badass Pantera female—been so captivated by him—his eyes, his lips, his scent—that she had felt nothing when he'd wrapped her up in…

Howling, she again strained against the bindings. What the fuck was this? Colorless, thin like pasta, but strong as iron. Cursing, she thrashed and thrashed. Never had she been so disgusted with herself.

When she found him, he was going to pay. Slow and bloody. And she would find him.

Fuck, she missed her cat.

Chapter Four

Sixteen. The number of safe houses he had acquired and set up within the United States alone. Not that they stayed under his control for very long. A year, at most. Buying and selling had become a full-time job. One that his lawyer—the only human he even remotely trusted—had taken over nearly three years ago. The main requirement for a property was to be remote. Impossible to get to. Tucked away.

This one was no different.

Outside the wall of windows he'd retracted the moment he'd stepped inside the house, the ocean crashed hard and aching against the rocks. The rhythm soothed him but it also reminded him of the constant that was his relationship with the Pantera. Pull away, return. Pull away, return. Would he ever truly escape them?

His belly growled, and he left the living room and headed for the kitchen. The four-room beach cottage looked wind and sea battered from the exterior, but inside, the home was fully decked out. The best of the best. He'd learned well from his former family.

He opened the fridge and stared. As usual, and like every other safe house, it was fully stocked. But nothing called to him. He closed the door and opened the freezer.

Raphael needed to give the fuck up already. He knew Simon wouldn't survive going back there. Even for an hour. He was one of only a few who knew and understood. But he didn't seem to give a shit. Granted, Simon had heard what was happening in the Wildlands—how dire things had become with the attack and with all the poor, damaged lab rats emerging. But he could do nothing for them. He had zero to offer. If anything, with his...deficiency, he'd add to the problem.

Grabbing the vodka and a tall glass, he poured himself a shot. Then another, as he stood against the island. Truly, alcohol was pointless. Never did dick to him—but did that stop him from trying? Nah. He was on a mission. Something, anything to get rid of his frustration over Raph and the memory of the red-haired puma female who was permanently burned on his retinas. He'd never been sent one like her. Stunning, sexy, a little scary...

A smile and a soft growl exited his throat. Which turned into a stilted laugh because he'd believed that sound—one brought forward from an animal's hunger—gone from him after all these years.

He was just pouring himself a third shot when a sharp scent assaulted his nostrils. Growling, turning into it, only a shock of red met his gaze before his head blasted with pain, his legs gave out beneath him, and his vision went dark. Cursing, teeth clenched, he reached for the counter, but only grasped air.

No!

Fuck! Impossible...

It was his last thought before blackness ripped through him and he was gone.

* * * *

Simon struggled within himself. Every time he seemed to find consciousness, he was pulled back to the bottom of the ocean, reaching the surface once again, an unattainable goal. Slight panic blanketing him, he persevered. Grave determination and fierce anger fueling him, he pushed himself up once more and finally, *finally* broke through. *Ahhhh...yes—sunlight!* Gulping the fresh air, he was relieved to be alive. But instantly on alert. For another attack—danger.

Or, in this case, for a very talented Hunter.

One who had, Simon mused, his head still buzzing from the painful intensity of his return trip to consciousness, stripped off his clothes and had his wrists and ankles tied to the four bedposts.

His fists clenched. His feet flexed.

Fuck.

He was secured too damn well. *Was that rope from his garage?*

"You snore."

The Hunter. Her voice. It made his skin hum with instant awareness.

His nostrils widening, he inhaled deeply. And that scent. He turned and spotted her sitting in one of the leather chairs a few feet from his bed, her back to the fading light of the afternoon sky. The French doors, which were open behind her, carried the full force of the ocean breeze, which was flipping the striped gray curtains back and forth in a wild fashion.

How long had he been out?

How long had she been sitting there, watching him.

Eyes narrowed, he stared at her. "How did you—" he began.

Her full mouth kicked up at the corners. "You think Raphael would send an amateur?" That smile widened. "The best tracker in the Wildlands, pretty boy."

Pretty boy… He didn't think he liked that. Especially coming from her. "And now that you've found me—?"

"And captured you," she added.

"And got me naked."

She shrugged. "Just making it a little harder for you to escape."

Oh, female, you're definitely making it harder…

He arched a brow at her. "How do you plan to get me out of here?"

"If I told you that—"

"You'd have to kill me?"

Her smile grew momentarily genuine. "No. But I would have to knock you out again."

It was his turn to smile. "Oh, kitten, that'll never happen. I promise you."

Instead of responding with one of her signature biting quips, she stood up and went over to the side of the bed. Her eyes moved down his body. Slowly. Irritatingly slowly. Pausing only when she reached his groin, then only waiting until his cock twitched and swelled slightly before dragging them upward.

What. The. Hell…

Maybe he'd underestimated this one.

Standing so close, yet not close enough to touch—or be touched. Heat assaulted him, and his hands formed fists once more. What was her plan? To torture him before she tried to get him back to the Wildlands? Was this payback for his containment of her in his dressing room?

"What color is your cat?" she asked, her eyes lifting to meet his. They were a strange blue at the moment. Pale, yet undeniably stormy. They made him anxious. Hungry. For her…for her hands on—

"Did you hear me, male?" she demanded.

Barely. His lust was clouding his hearing.

"I bet you're dark gray," she said. "Thick and glossy. I bet…your eyes turn the color of gunmetal when you shift."

Shift. The word slammed into his brain, making him slow, falter. What was she saying? Something about his…cat. Its color, its eyes…

The lust bled from his body, and he captured her gaze with more guarded, serious eyes. *Back to reality.* "So. Female. What's the plan here? Are they coming to fetch me instead? Raphael? The Hunters?"

But she wasn't done with her inspection or her questions. "How long has it been since you shifted? Do you miss it?" Her tongue slipped out and lapped at her upper lip. "I've been in this body less than a day and I'm going crazy. I can't imagine how you suffer."

Less than a day? Goddess, had Raphael sent him a feral Pantera? Was the Suit that big of a prick?

Stubborn female, meet even more stubborn male. "What time do they get here?" he pushed back. "Shame you needed your posse to help you. That you couldn't handle it alone. Handle *me* alone." His eyes flashed. "Thought you were the best of the best."

Her reaction was unexpected, to say the least. Instead of a verbal comeback or a sneer, growl, or snap, she reached for the rope around his left ankle and played with the fringe gently, almost thoughtfully. Then, after a moment, she brushed her fingers over his skin. Just a whisper of her fingers. He hissed. Tried to fight against the heat that gripped his belly and his groin. *I'm in control,* she seemed to be saying. Oh, yeah, that's exactly what she was saying—her fingers dragging upward now, over his calf, his knee…

The lust rushed back like a demon wanting to possess his body. His hard, trembling, hungry body.

"I'd say I'm handling you pretty well," she said softly, her fingers moving further, her nails gazing the skin of his thigh.

Simon growled a curse, his hips lifting without his consent as she paused inches from his now marble-hard erection.

What the fuck was she playing at? Forget payback. This was something else entirely… Raphael's desperation? The female's hatred for him?

Or worse, her desire?

The questions died in his mind as she suddenly pulled her hand away and left the bedside for the door.

Growling, snarling, he struggled against the ropes binding him. His cock hard, his blood desperate for sex, he was in no mood to be gentle or even subtle. "Where the fuck are you going, female?"

Her hand now wrapping the door handle, she called, "I'll be back."

"Alone?" he demanded.

She didn't answer him. Just turned out the light and left the room. Just as he'd done to her a few hours earlier.

Chapter Five

Tryst paced the kitchen floor. *Shit, shit, shit.* She was going full rogue here. The mission was to bring the male in. Done. Period. And it would've been so easy. Drugged, in the car, snoring away—next stop, Wildlands.

Instead, she'd stripped him, tied him to the bed and gone over every inch of him. Each scar, the waves of muscle on his belly, the tattoos on his scalp... After an hour, she'd thought better of it, caged her curiosity, not to mention her lust, and started to untie him. But then he'd said something. In his drugged sleep. Something that had made her both delay her plans and stay out of communication with Parish and Raphael. Neither one knew she had the male in her custody. She'd meant to contact them after securing him, hadn't wanted them to know she'd fucked up and allowed him to get away.

But those words had arrowed straight to her soul. Gutted her. Made her pine—not pity. Because if it was true...everything inside her—everything that snarled and stalked and loved the feel of the bayou sun on her belly—demanded that she help him... Fix him...

Fuck him.

The impulsive thought came out of nowhere and crashed into her brain—not to mention other warm, cavernous spaces as well. She was Pantera, belonged in the most savage parts of the Wildlands. She mated with those in their fur as well as out. She was as close to puma as—

Her breath hitched as she was suddenly yanked back and slammed against— Was that a brick wall or a male chest?

"How long ago did you call them, female?" Simon growled near her ear.

Her body seized with heat and adrenaline. Where had her instincts, her sense of smell... Where had it all gone?

"Answer me," he demanded, pulling her even tighter against him. Against his naked body.

Tryst snarled at the sensations coursing through her, at the unmitigated need that coiled in her belly. "Impossible," she uttered with lusty menace. "I tied those ropes—"

"Not tight enough, kitten," he said, cutting her off, punctuating his words by pressing his lips to the shell of her ear.

Her breathing went shallow, yet she continued to fight. "Didn't think to throw on some clothes before coming out here?" she said, feeling his erect cock nestled between her ass cheeks.

"I assumed you liked me this way," he whispered on a soft laugh. Making her shiver. Making her nipples tighten. Such a strange, yet not unwelcome feeling in human form.

"What is your name, female?" he demanded.

Heat was building inside her. Her lips felt dry. Her sex, wet. "Jane," she forced.

He growled at the lie.

"Sally," she said through gritted teeth. She couldn't give in to this. To him. To herself.

"Try again."

"Fine," she rasped. "It's Bitch."

In one swift movement, she sent her head back into his jaw. The sound of bone hitting bone electrified her. Simon grunted in pain and released her slightly. But it was enough for her to whirl around and try to get in another shot. This time with her fist. But the male's reflexes hadn't suffered being out of the Wildlands. Lower lip cut and bleeding, stormy blue eyes raging with ire, his grip on her only tightened further. And his growl...it was fierce and sharp, like a blade.

Crushed against his chest now, her breathing labored, she stared up at him.

"Name," he snarled.

Fine. What did it matter anyway? He'd find it out eventually. Chin jacked up, she said in a clear voice, "Tryst."

Nostrils flaring, his eyes never left hers. He was staring, assessing—reading. "Yes. There it is." His tongue darted out and lapped at the blood on his lip. "Now, *Tryst,* what game are you playing? Why was I naked and tied to my bed? Why aren't I crossing the border right now in one of the cars Jean-Baptiste no doubt loaned you, still fast asleep from the knockout you served me? Why isn't Parish smashing down my door this very second?"

"Takes time," she lied quickly. "Besides, he's not that fast when he's out of his cat form."

"Female," he warned. "You better tell me the truth." He lowered his head, studied her mouth, then lifted his eyes to hers. They were dark and narrowed. "You haven't told anyone where we are, have you?"

Goddess, he could read her well. Too well. And she was not just a closed book, but a locked one. Or believed herself to be. Maybe that was why Raph wanted him. What other talents did he have? Her belly stirred at the question.

His chin lifted. "Why?"

"I'll tell you if you tell me why you continually refuse to go back to the Wildlands." She arched one eyebrow. "What are you avoiding there? What made you leave? Or who?"

He looked stunned by her words, but his grip on her never lessened. "You first."

"Hell no."

"Don't trust me, female?"

Her lips twitched. "Is that a serious question?"

His jaw was working hard now, tightening. The movement was doing something to her. *He* was doing something to her. His lip was still bleeding and she wanted to swipe at it with her tongue. She wanted to taste him, feel the softness of his lips. What the fuck was wrong with her? She didn't react this way to anyone—not in her cat form or out of it. She wasn't capable of it. Refused it. She'd made the vow long ago—no one was going to control her...ever. Not her feelings, her needs, her hungers. She took. She demanded. Gave, too, but only because it granted her pleasure.

"Goddess, female," Simon uttered. "Stop whatever it is you're doing before I..."

Her eyes lifted to meet his. A raging sea under gray clouds. "What?"

"You want to fuck me."

She swallowed. "Probably."

"You don't deny it?" he said on a soft growl.

"Why should I?"

His face was a mask of confusion and lust as he tried to figure her out.

"It's true," she continued, her body weary of the fight, yet it hummed with a strange, new need. "I'm curious. I'm aroused. I'm—"

"Honest," he finished for her.

She slipped her hand around his waist and palmed his ass. Then squeezed. Perfect. Tight. Fingers sinking into the muscular flesh until she heard him groan. Her eyes clung to his. "You've been out of the Wildlands and living with coy humans too long, male. Always having to pretend they don't want what they want. What their bodies crave." Growling at herself, her needs, him, she released him. "Doesn't mean I'll do anything about it though."

"I'd call that doing something." He ground himself against her and hissed. "It's sure as fuck done something to me."

She tried to slow her pulse, tried to ignore the wetness between her legs. "Just wanted to see if a deserter like you has lost the muscle of a Pantera male."

"And?" he said mockingly, knowing full well that both his cock and his body were a solid wall.

Hell, if it was possible, he was even more toned and hard then the Hunters she worked with daily. "Are you going to let me go?" she asked him. "Or do I need to bloody your nose this time?"

"You sure you want that, Tryst?" he asked, his eyes filled with lusty humor now.

She grabbed his waist and thrust herself back. This time, he didn't hold her. This time, he let her go. Five feet away or so. Just far enough to see what was right in front of her. She gasped, couldn't help it, then promptly hated herself for it. The male's erect cock...it was...huge. Long and thick and proud, and if on display would be the desire of any true puma female.

She licked her lips.

"Hungry, Tryst?"

She forced her eyes up, though they didn't want to. "I could eat."

He grinned, his nostrils flaring. "Well, this is certainly an interesting situation. Can't say I've ever been in one like it." He raised a brow. "You eat meat, I assume?"

Her lips twitched. This male… So tempting. "Always."

He nodded casually, though every inch of him was on alert, ready to pounce. But then, like a switch being turned off, something happened...in his eyes, his expression. All playful, sexual humor was gone.

"I'm going to throw on some jeans," he said, his voice heavily controlled. "I'll be back. Make us some dinner. We should talk. Find out why I'm still here and not on my way to the Wildlands."

Not sure I can or want to answer that question, she mused, watching him walk away. *Oh, hot fucking damn, what a view.* She'd never felt desire like this. And the worst bit? For the first time since she'd crossed the border into the human world, she didn't miss her cat.

* * * *

Simon watched her lift the glass to her lips. She had a gorgeous mouth. Heavy, dark pink. No straw-thin model could even come close to the lean-muscled strength and fierce sexuality of a Pantera female. But this one took that notion to an entirely different level.

"You're not drinking," he observed.

Her eyes held his. No answer.

He laughed softly. "Spiking booze is your thing, female. Not mine."

She continued to stare at him across the small dining table, just off the living room, her long red hair gently blowing across her shoulders in the cross breeze of the ocean out the floor-to-ceiling glass doors behind him.

"Trust me," he said. "If I wanted out of here, away from you, it would've happened hours ago. Like after I chewed through those ropes."

The wine came away from her lips and her eyes narrowed. "Not possible."

Grinning, he reached for her glass, then gave her his. "You don't know me, Tryst. Anything about me. What I'm capable of."

"I know you're a Suit," she countered.

"Was," he corrected. "A hundred years ago." *Or so it feels like.*

"I know you were the youngest Suit they'd ever let go out into the field."

He inhaled sharply. "I was an ambitious little fucker." *Desperate to prove myself. Desperate for anyone to see my worth.*

"Your family was okay with that?" she asked. "You taking off, working with grown Pantera, barely out of cubhood?"

The word sizzled inside him, heating his blood. *Family.* But he crushed the feeling instantly. Just as he had for decades. As he always would. "They were thrilled." *To get rid of me. To not have to look at me.*

"Lucky," she said, taking a sip of the wine. "My parents are overly involved in my life. They pretty much think I'm the weirdest Pantera ever."

"Why's that?"

"I live in my puma most of the time. Don't go to visit them very often. I like being by myself." She held up her fork. "See. Weird."

"Doesn't sound weird to me."

She laughed. "What does it sound like?"

Heaven. He pointed at her plate. "How's the steak. Bloody enough for you?"

"It's damn good, pretty boy." She regarded him. "Now, answer the question—what does it sound like?"

Stubborn. He leaned in. "That maybe you don't play well with others."

She laughed again and pointed her fork at him. "You know, if you weren't a deserter, I might like you." She stabbed a thick, juicy piece and stuffed it into her mouth.

"And if you weren't an annoying, persistent, and slightly scary Hunter who refused to face the reality that she isn't getting her man this time around, I might like you."

"Oh, darlin'," she drawled. "I'm getting my man. I am so getting my man."

It was his turn to laugh. A real, hearty, Pantera male laugh. From the gut. And possibly even from the heart. It was a rare sound, coming from him. But this female...she was rare, and she seemed to call it forth. This female, who was only here to capture and return him to the one place on earth he refused to go.

"So, that first job you took," she asked, ripping a piece of bread in half. "Was it your last?"

"No."

When he didn't explain further, she cocked her head to the side. "Come on. Sharing is caring, male."

"Eat your potatoes. I mashed those bad boys myself."

"Look, you don't have to tell me why you walked away, just tell me...when?"

He put his fork down. She was relentless. "Four years in."

"And you never went back?"

"No."

"Not even to see your family?"

The question grated on the iron he'd erected around his heart. "What's with you and family?" he growled.

"I don't know. Seems like a normal question."

Of course it was. For anyone but him—and for anyone but them. She wasn't his date. Someone to share with and confide in, as if he did that anyway. This was a second out of time, wrong, right, impossible. His appetite gone, he pushed back his chair and stood up. Without words, he offered her his hand.

She stared at it. "What's this all about?"

"I like this song, okay?"

She glanced around. "Is there music playing?"

His lips twitched. "You don't hear it?" Without waiting for an answer, he reached for her and pulled her from her chair and into his arms.

She didn't try and resist him, but she was taken by surprise at first. Her eyes clinging to his, she slowly placed her arm on his shoulder, her fingers resting lightly at the nape of his neck. The sensation of closeness, of her against him in such a normal, real manner made his gut tighten. Made other parts of him tighten as well.

One auburn eyebrow lifted and she asked, "Is it the ocean? Is that your music?"

His lips curved into a smile. "Maybe."

She laughed softly, femininely. "This is…interesting," she remarked, trying to follow him as he gently swayed.

It wasn't that she was awkward as she moved. More, hesitant. "You've never danced with a male before, have you?"

"Like I said, I'm rarely out of my cat."

"Weird."

"Hey!" she shot back, her laugh turning playful and girlish now as her hand closed around the back of his neck.

He laughed too. "I'm kidding." Then he lowered his head and whispered, "I like it."

She rolled her eyes.

"It's true." The mirth suddenly died away and was replaced by the sobering feeling that something was happening there, in the air around them, between them. Something far more complicated than lust or a cat-and-mouse chase and capture. "I like that you haven't done this with anyone else. See." He arched a brow. "I still have my Pantera male instincts."

"Yes, I believe you do."

Her eyes remained locked with his as they moved. As the ocean crashed against the rocks outside the doors. Clearly, she felt it too and it sobered her as well. What did it mean? That she hadn't completed her mission and dragged him back to the Wildlands? And what did it mean that he wasn't running?

"Why do you think you prefer your cat to…this form?" he asked. He couldn't imagine. For a few reasons. One being that this form was…spectacular.

"It's my comfort, I guess. I feel…content, at peace."

"So you understand, then."

Her brow furrowed. "What?"

He stopped moving, and his eyes bore into hers. "Being away from the Wildlands is my comfort, Tryst. I feel content. At peace."

She considered this for a moment, her expression a palette of conflicting emotions. "No one's asking you to return for good."

"No one's asking at all."

"Raphael's our leader, Simon."

It was the first time she'd used his name, instead of "pretty boy" or "male." Or it was the first time he recalled it. Either way, the word on her lips burned and hummed inside him. "He's not my leader. Not anymore."

She didn't like that answer at all. Her body stiffened, and her stubborn face was set once again. "You have to go back."

"Not happening, female."

"I have a mission."

"You already failed it."

Her lips parted and she growled at him.

"Look at us, for fuck's sake."

Her expression frosted over and she said in a deadly voice, "I never fail."

"I believe it," he said easily, then leaned in and whispered close to her ear. "We both know what you're capable of, kitten. If you wanted me incapacitated right now, you probably could manage it." *And if I wanted to escape, I would've already done it.*

A soft growl vibrated in her throat. "No probably about it, male."

"Don't get me wrong, it's incredibly sexy." Slow and gentle, he licked the shell of her ear. When she shivered, he grinned. "My point is, we're both here because we want to be."

"For now," she breathed.

"Yes," he agreed. "For now."

Several long seconds ticked by and she remained still, though her breathing grew more labored, in sync now with the rhythm of the ocean against the rocks. Goddess, this female intrigued him. Her brain, her brawn, not to mention the raw sexuality she displayed. She was like a forbidden fruit, and he wanted to taste her skin again. The curve of her ear, maybe the lobe, maybe the band of muscle on her neck that housed the beat of her heart. For starters, that is. Every inch of him was humming with need.

"Tryst—" He barely got her name from his lips before she drove him backward and slammed him against the wall.

"I didn't fail," she ground out, her chin lifted, her mouth impossibly close to his. "I postponed."

His own pulse knocking against his ribs in a frantic tattoo, he grinned down at her. "Okay."

Her hand slipped between them and she ripped at the button of his jeans, then yanked down his fly. "But I will get you back there, make no mistake about it."

His nostrils flared as her fingers dove into the waistband and threaded through his hair. "I'd never make the mistake of underestimating you, Tryst. You're in control here."

"Liar," she said with a wicked grin, then wrapped her hand around his rigid cock, which had sprung free the second she'd pulled his zipper down.

A snarl ripped from his lips at her possessive touch, but his eyes remained fixated on her. "Fine. We're mutually out of control, how's that?"

She cursed as she squeezed his erection, shook her head in frustration. "It's crazy. It's not me. But I can't stop thinking about this… You…" She started to stroke him, long, possessive strokes, up and down, pausing for only a second or two to run her thumb across the head.

"Tryst," he groaned, knocking his head back against the wall to keep his sanity. Her touch was fire and ice and sweet and soft, and he never wanted it to stop. "Fuck…"

"No," she said breathlessly in reply, dropping to her knees and dragging his jeans down with her. "Not yet."

Chapter Six

She gazed at it. At him. Almost lovingly.

Long, hard, pink.

Mine.

Taking a male into her mouth was foreign to her. Of course, she'd heard about it. Even seen it. Pantera weren't shy creatures. A bed of grass or the shore of the bayou—even up against a tree—served as a fine rutting space. But she'd never done it. Never even thought about it. To her, sex with a male was an animal's reaction to a base need. An exchange. Most of the time on all fours.

But with him...*this* male, it was like she wanted to see everything, every inch of him, explore him with her tongue. Taste him, scent him. Know what his heart sounded like inside his chest as he grew more and more excited. And all in her female skin.

What was this?

This strange hunger?

Poised on her knees, her hands stacked, fingers wrapping around his incredible cock, she lowered her head and took him into her mouth. All the way. Not stopping until he was at the back of her throat. Then she inhaled deeply. She liked him there. Deep inside her. Consuming him.

And the sound that erupted from him as she did told her he liked it too. More than liked it, she guessed.

"Tryst," he growled. "You're going to send me off, over the fucking edge."

Perfect. Slowly, she began to move, drawing him out, then sucking him back in. Again and again, slowly and deliberately, reveling in the grunts and growls, following the rhythm of his body.

A salty taste met her tongue and she moaned softly.

Drawing back, holding him in her hands, she looked up at him. He was pressed into the wall, hands fisted. His face and neck were filled with tension. His lips were parted and his nostrils were flared. He was breathing heavily. She wished he was naked. Wished she could see every bit of him.

"I love the way you taste," she said.

He groaned. "Fuck, Tryst. You're killing me."

"No, male. You're very much alive." She leaned in and lapped at the head of his wet cock. *Yum.* She could live off him. "And you are Pantera. Every inch of you. Your scent, your taste, your sounds." Her eyes closed and she dipped her tongue inside the slit. "Mmmmm," she whispered before taking him into her mouth once again.

As he cursed into the ocean breeze, she reached around and grabbed his ass, which was as hard as his cock.

Mine.

She felt like a female possessed.

No, she realized, stunned. She felt like her cat. On edge, ready, humming to attack, so hungry.

Her fingers wrapping the base of him, she let him take the lead, thrust into her mouth at his own pace. All she did was take. His pre-come, his pounding strokes. She couldn't get enough. And when he warned her, let her know he was on the brink and he would flood her if she remained, not only did she stay, but she squeezed his ass and pressed him closer still.

A snarl broke in the salty air that rushed into the small dining room and spurred on several deep thrusts and the pounding of fists into the wall behind him. No doubt he was leaving marks, but neither of them paused to look.

"Tryst." The word was guttural on his lips as he came, hard and hot and abundant into her mouth.

And like the thirsty cat she was, she drank him down.

What was this? she asked herself again. Lust? Maybe. Curiosity? Possibly. A need for something more than she'd ever had, or wanted, or thought existed?

She eased back, wiped her mouth and tried to stand. But Simon was already upon her, over her, guiding her back onto the rug.

"Don't get up," he said, his eyes flashing with unclaimed desire. "Don't you dare."

As she watched, he pulled off his shirt, tossed his jeans over her head, then started in on her. It was the strangest sensation, yet felt incredibly right. With each inch of skin he exposed, the sea air would coat it—skin, not fur. It tingled, heated, then cooled.

"You are breathtaking, female."

So engrossed in the new sensation, she hadn't realized Simon was sitting back on his haunches, staring at her. His eyes were glazed with lust and admiration as he took in every inch of her nakedness. What would it feel like? she wondered. His skin; his strong, hard skin pressed up against hers? Rubbing against hers?

But he didn't touch her as he moved over her, holding himself up on his hands. His eyes were fixed on her eyes now, their mouths close together, breath commingling. He was going to kiss her, press his lips to hers. It was wildly erotic. Granted, she'd been taken—as a cat, she'd been taken. But never had she been face-to-face with a male as he made love to her mouth.

It was too intimate.

When breath collided with breath, a trust, a vulnerability, was formed

"Tryst," he whispered, his eyes closing as his mouth covered hers in a slow, drugging, perfectly wet kiss. "I don't know what the fuck is happening to me, but—"

"I love it," she uttered, tipping her chin up, wanting to get closer.

He smiled. "Me too, kitten. Goddess, me too."

Once again, he kissed her, capturing her in a series of brutal, then tender, assaults. His tongue was hungry and determined to play with hers, and she happily obliged. This was dreamy, she mused, making out with the very male she should be returning to the Wildlands. Perfection. And she never wanted it to stop.

She wrapped her arms around his neck and whispered against his lips, "Do you taste yourself when you kiss me? Salty and sweet all at the same time."

He groaned with the query and she felt his cock turn to stone against her belly.

"I taste me, you, us," he said before capturing her mouth again in a series of sensual kisses that left her breathless. "It's all I want. More of this, of you. Goddess, you're sweet, Tryst. I'm addicted already."

And with that, he abandoned her mouth and started to move. Down. Capturing her neck, sucking at the band that housed her pulse, then biting at her collarbone. Tryst let her head fall back, let her fingers dive into his thick black hair. Relishing in the movement, the beautiful assault to her hot skin.

It was like he was everywhere at once. His heavily muscled body and limbs on her, moving on her. And his mouth and tongue tasting every inch of skin he could find. A gasp tore from her throat as he found her right breast and suckled the nipple deep into his mouth.

Shards of painful, wonderfully painful heat ripped through her sex and she canted her hips. Goddess, this was heaven. How had she not known or cared? Was she waiting for him? For this male?

Was he the one, the only one, who could bring such deep, glorious feeling out of her?

Her fingers pressing into his scalp, she forced him to her left breast. He chuckled softly but did as she wished, his warm breath making her pussy cry with arousal. He was magic, the way he licked and sucked and tortured her with the tip of his nose. And she was madness. Thrusting her hips, calling out, begging for more, him, everything.

Suddenly, she realized he'd moved. Down. Kissing his way. Nibbling at her hipbones, opening her thighs and pressing her knees back. "What are you doing?" she demanded in an utterly breathless tone.

"Kissing you," he said with ferocity, his eyes fixated on her pussy, spread wide for his seemingly utter delight.

"You're going to lick me?"

He glanced up, his eyes so hooded and dark her heart jumped in her breast. "Oh, yes."

She inhaled sharply. "Bite me?"

"If you want me to."

"I didn't bite you."

"That's okay." His grin widened. It was the grin of a cat with a plate of delicious milk in sight. "Next time."

A response never crossed her lips, because the moment he lowered his head and nuzzled between the lips of her pussy with his nose, Tryst was gone.

Floating.

Alive.

* * * *

Simon inhaled. Breathed the scent of her into his parched lungs. He refused to think, analyze, do anything that would draw his mind from her. From this moment.

As the wind rushed in through the doors to his right, Simon took her in. Pink, flushed skin, pale blue eyes alive with fire and trained on him, on his every move. Yards of thick red hair spread out around her perfect face. Chest rising and falling, quickly, as she anticipated his touch.

Spreading her lips, he dropped his head and licked her, from her entrance to the hood of her clit. The soft groan that followed made his dick impossibly harder and his tongue desperate to play, and to bring her to climax. Careful not to overstimulate her, he flicked the swelling bud. Back and forth. And with every flick, she released a cry of need, canted her hips.

He brought his fingers up and played with the entrance to her sex, circling, coating each digit in her cream. Hunger drowned him, made him mad with lust, and he sank those fingers into his mouth and sucked. Goddess, she tasted like heaven. How was this happening? How had the perfect female been sent to him?

A whisper of worry trod through his mind, but he sent it away. They were both here. Had chosen to be here. With each other. That was all that mattered right now.

"Come for me, Tryst," he said, slipping two fingers inside her and slowly thrusting. "I want to watch you. Every second. As your body takes me, takes what I'm doing to you."

His eyes on her still, he circled her clit with his tongue, then suckled it into his mouth. Over and over he worked this pattern as he pumped his fingers inside her. So deep he felt lost. So wet the sound of them echoed over the ocean.

She was close, the walls of her pussy clenching and vibrating and creaming around his fingers. He couldn't wait, wait to hear her scream—wait to drink her come as she drank his.

"It's too much, male," she suddenly cried out. "Goddess, please!"

Her words halted him firm, and he looked up. "What's wrong?"

She lifted her head, gazed at him with eyes wide and filled with sexual madness, skin flushed and vibrating with arousal. "It's too much."

"Too much of what, *ma chère?* Talk to me. Tell me what you need."

"Too much heat, too much good, too much I want. But it'll never be enough. I'll never have enough."

Simon stifled a smile. A stunned smile. What was happening here? It was as if she'd never… His smile died. Had she never come before? No…that would be impossible—at least with her own hand. What about at the hand of another male? Fuck, he refused to even acknowledge the possibility. She was to cry out from him—only him. That's all he was willing to grant at that moment.

His gaze moved over her. Her pink skin, glistening with sweat, hands fisted on the rug, her breathing labored, and her expression…confusion mixed with animal-like hunger.

"Do you want me to stop, Tryst?" he asked.

"No," she growled at him, baring her teeth. "Do it and I'll bite you. And you won't like it."

His mouth twitched. "Then stop thinking. Let yourself feel. Even if it's too much. Feel all the good, all the heat…"

He said nothing more. His fingers started to pump inside her once again, and he tucked back into his feast. Licking, suckling, flattening his tongue and moving with each thrust of her hips. She was mewling now, like a kitten, creaming around him so fitfully the insides of her thighs were soaked.

Maintaining the pace, Simon growled into the air. *Mine. Mine. Mine.* She was shaking—her hands, her legs, her pussy.

"Goddess!" she screamed, her hips slamming up and down as he thrust inside her. "Yes! Yes, please."

She came in a roar of sound, crying, keening, mewling, sighing. And Simon took it all in, with his mouth, his tongue, his eyes and, Goddess help him, his heart. It was truly the most beautiful thing he'd ever seen.

She was the most beautiful sight.

This Pantera.

This female he knew, in his gut, belonged to him.

Chapter Seven

"This wasn't at all how I thought my mission would go," Tryst said on a sigh, nuzzling deeper into Simon's shoulder as around them night fell and the moon glowed brilliantly over a calm sea. She'd never felt so content, so at peace.

Not even in the Wildlands, or in her cat.

"Well, if it's any consolation, female," he said, kissing the top of her head, "you did capture me. Just not in the way you originally planned."

Laughing softly, she came up on her elbow and stared at him. This ridiculously gorgeous male. This pretty boy who, with every touch, every sound, every movement, couldn't mask the warrior beneath. The loner and rebel who had left his family, barely out of cubhood, to take a power position as a Suit. He was cunning and clever, and had the most wicked of tongues.

He was hers.

If only in an alternate universe.

He brought his hand up and sank his fingers into her hair. "What are you thinking, female? Your eyes won't tell me a thing."

Oh, no, she couldn't let him know her possessive thoughts. "I've never…been with a male outside of my cat form."

Surprise registered on his handsome face. "You haven't?"

She shook her head. "Never even thought about it."

"But you knew others did—"

"Of course," she jumped in quickly. "Hell, as a Hunter I've walked in on a few of them. It just wasn't something that interested me."

"And now?" He said the words softly, as if he wasn't sure he wanted to hear the answer.

"Now," she said with a wicked smile, dropping her head and planting a slow, dragging kiss on his lips, "I think I like it. A lot. I think I may need to do it again sometime."

It was like a wave of hot, snarling wind rushed her, and in less than a second, she was on her back and he was poised over her. Nostrils flaring, upper lip curling, he growled, "Another male touches you and he will find breathing a difficult—"

"Hey," she cut him off harshly. "I was talking about you, you idiot."

The mask of animal ire evaporated instantly. "Oh."

She rolled her eyes. "*Oh.* Males. I suggest we touch and taste each other again, maybe more, and all you have to say is 'Oh.'"

His eyes cleared and a smile cut his fine features. He bent his head and took her mouth in the hottest, sweetest, most drugging kiss ever. "Tryst," he breathed.

"You are just like Parish and Lian with their mates," she uttered against his mouth. "Angry and possessive one moment, wanting to kiss and rut the next."

He bit her lip.

She gasped.

"Mates don't rut, kitten," he said.

Her heart lurched. She didn't want to go there—question the use of that word—in her head or anywhere else. But she couldn't help herself. He was poised overover her, his eyes drinking her in, his mouth ready and saying things that made her ache with want. "What do they do then?"

He pressed his expanding erection against her sex. "Fuck."

Letting her legs fall open a little wider, she sucked air between her teeth. She wanted him. Deep inside her. Fucking her. Yes, lots of fucking. She smiled to herself despite the hot bands of tension running through her belly.

"Have you taken a mate?" she asked him. "Outside the Wildlands?"

He kissed her neck. "No."

"That's good. I wouldn't like it."

He eased back so he could see her. "You're so honest. About your feelings, your past, your life."

"I have nothing to hide or be ashamed of."

"Of course not. I didn't mean it like that." He reached out and brushed a strand of hair off her breast, then followed it up with a kiss to her nipple. "I admire it, Tryst." Then he muttered, "Jealous of it, even."

Not understanding him, she cupped his face in her hands and held him steady, so their eyes locked. "You can be this way, too. Open, honest. No fear."

His gaze pulled from hers and she wondered at it. Did he not really believe that? Or was he hiding something too deep, too painful to release? She wondered perhaps if it had something to do with what he'd said in his sleep? What he'd lamented. Did he really believe it to be true? That he couldn't shift? That he had no cat within him? Never had...?

"Simon?" she said.

His eyes lifted. They were shuttered and wary. "Female?"

She brushed her thumb over his lower lip. "I see it in there, in your eyes."

Those eyes narrowed. "What do you see?"

"Your cat."

His expression turned fierce and he tried to pull away. But she held him fast. "Listen. Please. When you had your back against the wall, growling as I took you in my mouth, I saw it. When you had my legs over your head and you were eating me like a starving beast, I saw it."

"Tryst," he warned.

"And even now, hovering above me, your eyes fierce, I see it." She swallowed thickly. "I imagine it's a beautiful creature. Terrifying and cunning, like its master."

It must be caged inside him, she thought. Somewhere cavernous. Somewhere he couldn't access. No Pantera was born without a cat. That would be akin to saying one was born without a soul. And this male, he had a soul. It had spoken to hers, touched hers.

If given the time, she knew she could find it.

But time wasn't all that plentiful with them. And Simon's mood had turned from romantic and connected to hungry and wicked.

"You want to meet what's inside me, Tryst?" he asked, wrapping his arms around her and rolling them to the side so he was on his back and she was the one poised above. "Well, I want to meet what's inside you." And with those words, he lifted her up, held her there for a moment. Then slowly, achingly slowly, placed her down on his shaft.

Tryst inhaled sharply at the incredible invasion. Forgot everything she had been thinking and saying and only wanted *this*. Oh, yes, this was good.

Simon dragged his palms up her belly, over her ribs to her breasts, and Tryst just leaned into him. The ocean breeze at her back, she started to move. Back and forth. Back and forth. His eyes were on hers. Hers on his. And as she circled her hips, felt him touch that deepest, most sensitive flesh inside her, she understood. It wasn't just animal lust, a need for release. It wasn't rutting. It wasn't even fucking. Simon had got it wrong too. It was a connection. Between two beings. Souls colliding and swirling around each other, entering the other and changing them for good.

As if Simon had heard her thoughts, he sat up and wrapped his arms around her. For several moments, he didn't move. Just stayed locked to her.

"Do you see my cat now, Tryst?" he asked.

"Simon..."

"Do you see it?"

She reached up and brushed hair from his sweaty forehead. "I see it in everything you do."

He shook his head. "I don't know what you think you see, but it's no puma."

"What do you mean?" she began. "You don't truly think—"

He covered her mouth and kissed her. Deep and demanding. "No more...just, no more."

"Simon—"

"No more, kitten," he said, his tone resolute.

"Okay," she breathed. Later. Later she would talk with him, tell him what she'd heard him say...find out what he believed and why. But right now...

His lips were on hers again, and as he kissed her, Tryst let herself go. Let her mind fall apart.

"Hold on, female," he demanded, slowly thrusting into her again.

Heat pooled low in her belly and her breasts ached, her nipples tightening against his chest. He pushed into her like a male possessed, a male trying to rid himself of pain. Gain only pleasure and peace. Clinging to him, she kissed him and followed his rhythm until the heat was unbearable. Rising from her toes to her sex to her face, then returning to the very center of her once again.

When his hands found and cupped her ass, when he used her backside to grind even deeper inside her, her body shook and shivered. She came harder than ever before, racking groans, aching sex, and her teeth sinking into his powerful shoulder.

The latter sent him over the edge of madness. He was like a possessed creature. Manic. Driving into her like a demon as his fingers dug into her flesh. And then he growled the word...

"Mine."

And he exploded inside her.

It was cataclysmic. Shocking in its intensity. Tryst trembled, tears behind her eyes. *Tears!* Unheard of. She wasn't emotional. She wasn't soft and sweet and tender-hearted. She was a female who could break a male's arm without a thought or a care if he didn't give her the information she required.

But Simon had changed her.

Inside and out.

For moments—or was it hours? Days? A week? She didn't know, but she clung to him, boneless, her mind lost to her.

What was it, again...? Why was she here? What was she supposed to be doing? Her eyes closed and she exhaled the world. It helped some. But there was still a Hunter residing beneath her skin and inside her brain. It took the form of a very small red light that flickered on and off. A warning signal. Stay awake. Think... Do your job.

The mission.

You are a Hunter.

This is your hunted.

Suddenly, she was being lifted. The wind off the ocean was brushing her skin, making her shiver. But then warmth overtook the cold. Simon had curled her into his arms. And they were moving...leaving the room.

Simon.

Oh, it felt so good to be in his arms, to be cared for. To be able to be vulnerable. Why had she never wanted it? Sought it out?

"Where?" she rasped, her voice gone from the cries and growls, the screams and the rapid breathing.

"Taking you to bed, *ma chère*," he said. "To sleep."

Sleep. With him. Against him. Skin to skin.

Her male.

The red light flickered once again.

Sheets, cool and soft. And Simon's hard body beside her. *Red light, be gone. You have no place here.*

"Tryst," he whispered against her hair once he'd tucked her into his side.

"Simon," she whispered back, allowing herself to be completely at another's mercy for the first time in her life.

And, her mind warned her as her consciousness started to recede, the last.

* * * *

Simon growled in his sleep, famished yet satiated. They'd had little rest, had "fucked" twice more after a short nap, then dropped like stones into each other's arms. But that didn't stop him from wanting her again. Now.

A smile on his lips, he rolled over, reaching for her. But soft, warm female was not what he got.

"Hands off, asshole."

Flash-quick, Simon was up and awake and had his fingers wrapped around the neck of the male who had spoken—a male he knew all too well. Skull-shaved head and devious-as-shit green eyes.

"Michel," he ground out. *What the hell?* He glanced around, fingers still curled around the male's neck. *Fucking assholes.*

"Hey there, brother."

He turned back to the Suit and snarled at him. "Don't call me that. How long have I been out? And where's Tryst? Where did you…" The rest of the sentence died off. A quick, terrible death as events of the day came rolling back.

As quick as he'd pounced on the Michel, he released him and dropped into the seat of the limousine that was no doubt whisking him toward the one place on earth he never wanted to go again.

"Not going to finish what you started?" Michel asked him, rubbing his neck and chuckling. "Squeeze my throat until I pass out? Might be able to get the car to stop. Get out. Get away. Again."

"Fuck off," was all Simon said. All he had the energy for. Besides, what more was there? Didn't matter. After yesterday and last night...all that had been said and shared… He'd fucked the beautiful, ruthless Hunter, and now he was being fucked right back. He deserved it for allowing her to get inside his heart.

Play with his very soul.

"It's one hour, max," Michel told him, his tone holding zero pity. "You don't even have to see anyone. Just give Raphael what he wants and you're gone."

Eyes on the window, he flipped the Suit off.

"Fine. Be pissed. But you're still a Pantera whether you reject us or not. And that means something. We are family, kin. We care for each other, protect each other—"

Simon laughed bitterly. "The Pantera don't know dick about protection. Or care. Or respect. Or honor."

"Are we still talking about Raphael? Or is this about Tryst now?"

A low, feral snarl erupted from Simon's throat.

"Don't blame her," Michel said, his tone threaded with warning.

Eyes still trained on the world outside the window, Simon uttered, "Didn't I tell you to fuck off? I'm pretty sure I did."

"She was just doing her job. You understand that. Or you used to."

If the male spoke of Tryst one more time, Simon was going to lose his shit. Even now, his hands were twitching, desperate to find their way back to his neck. Pointing to the front of the limo, Simon barked, "Can't that asshole drive any faster? I want this over with."

"Wow." Michel sniffed. "After years of trying to get you back to the Wildlands, I can't believe I'm hearing you say that. You're seriously not going to try and escape this time?"

Simon's head came around fast, and his smile was as black and vicious as his heart. "No. You got me. Congrats." With a wink, he added, "One helluva weapon you used."

Michel's jaw worked with the insinuation, but he said no more. What was there to say anyway? It was done. And once Raphael had what he wanted, Simon would be gone—never to be their pawn again.

It would be his one and only stipulation.

Well, that and never again having to set his eyes on the female who'd betrayed him.

Chapter Eight

"I want to be here when you speak to him."

Raphael glanced up from his makeshift desk in his hastily built private office, located in the center of town, which was serving as temporary Headquarters during the rebuild. "I don't think so, Tryst."

"I'm sorry," she said, crossing her arms over her chest. "I think you've misunderstood me. I wasn't asking. I demand to be here."

His brow lifted over very critical gold/jade eyes. "You know who you're speaking to, don't you?"

"I do."

The leader of the Pantera took in her stubborn stance, her rigid jaw. "Go home, Tryst," he growled. "You've earned some rest, and clearly you need it."

She didn't move. He was wrong on that account. Dead wrong. She'd earned nothing. Except maybe the absolute hatred of the male she wanted more than anything in this world. She hadn't even earned the pleasure of being back in her cat. She hadn't shifted once since she crossed the border. And it wasn't for lack of trying. It was like the feline was rejecting her. And she hardly blamed it.

A sudden commotion outside drew her attention, Raphael's too. The door to the quickly produced space of four walls and a roof opened and two males entered.

"He's here, Raph," Roch said, his ice blue eyes surveying the room and landing on Tryst.

She didn't know the Suit all that well, but it was clear he wasn't too fond of her at the moment.

"What's she doing here?" he inquired brusquely. "He doesn't want to see her."

Standing beside Roch, another Suit, Michel, nodded. This one she knew a bit better. "Go, Tryst."

But really, it was too late. There was one door, and she'd have to pass him to get out. Not to mention that the moment she saw him, the moment her eyes landed on his tall, broad frame, his hands, his lips...his eyes, she would be utterly immobile. Even though he despised her. Even though she'd committed the worst offense one could commit against a lover. Even though she'd truly broken them.

Mine.

Those dark blue, stormy eyes hit her full force as he stalked into the office, heading straight for Raphael. "You're fucking kidding me with this, right?"

He was talking about her, and it cut to the bone.

"Tryst." The leader's voice was deadly now.

She swallowed hard. She'd never disobeyed a direct order, but this went beyond Pantera rule of law. This was about the heart. And a claiming. "I demand to stay."

Roch shook his head. "Hunters..."

She turned and flipped him off.

"On what grounds?" Raphael asked, every word a silent throttle.

"I don't give a shit about grounds," Simon said to Raphael, keeping his back to her. "I don't want her here. Deal's off if she stays."

Goddess, she despised his words, but pain lanced through her at his frigid tone. Even so, she held firm. "I'm staying. It's my right."

This time, Simon turned to face her. Nostrils flared, upper lip curled, he was a wondrous sight to behold. So male, so Pantera. Even in his hatred and revulsion, she felt his need for her. To strangle her or kiss her, it was so close a desire in that moment.

"You have no rights regarding me, female," he said seethingly. "Not now. Not ever."

"I'm afraid I do."

His eyes narrowed.

"Tryst, what the hell are you talking about?" Raphael demanded, sitting back in his chair.

Was she going to do this? Her cat pushed her onward. "Simon is my mate. He's claimed me. And I've claimed him. In blood."

The room went dead silent as every pair of eyes turned on Simon and remained.

* * * *

Simon wished to the Goddess that he could feel numb. It would be so much easier than the train wreck of emotions spiraling though him at the female's words.

No, her declaration.

First off, he hated seeing her. Her hair was down and wild, just as it had been in his bed. Her mouth was still swollen from his kisses, and her eyes were weary from choices she'd felt compelled to make. Choices that had damaged whatever bond they'd managed to create in the past day.

He turned back to Raphael and stated coldly, "She's not my mate."

"We were together last night," Tryst said.

He sniffed. "No different than any other night. Or any other female."

Roch's eyes widened and he glanced at Michel, who mouthed the word *Damn.*

"His boasting makes no difference to me or to the truth," she continued, the stubborn fighter Simon had come to know out in full force now. "This wasn't a casual rut—"

"Tryst," Raphael warned.

"Oh, yes, I shouldn't talk like that in front of all these innocent males." She snorted.

She was in her element now. Mocking and fierce. Goddess, Simon hated it. Hated her. Wanted her. Even now, as she stood there a traitor to him.

"I think if I tell you all the ways we were together yesterday, it would prove—"

"No," Simon ground out. "Are you going to stop this?" he said to Raphael. "You are still the leader of the Pantera, correct?"

"Hey, if the female needs to get the details off her chest," Michel started with a grin. But Simon silenced him with a feral glare.

Michel laughed. "Oh, sure. You're not mates at all. Recognize that look, Roch?"

"I do indeed," the Suit returned. "Every time I look in the mirror."

"Shut up. The both of you." Raphael sat back down, exhaled heavily. "We won't debate this further. If you were with her, Simon, and blood was drawn—"

"It was," Tryst assured him.

"You bit me!" Simon snarled.

"And you loved it."

Raphael banged his fist on the desk. "Clearly, there was some kind of claiming...she may stay."

"Fine," Simon muttered. "Whatever. I don't give a shit who hears. Tell me what you want, Raphael. Now, before I lose my fucking mind in here."

"Your parents."

The two words were like a punch to the jaw. A bleak coldness spread through him as he replayed them, icing his veins. "I haven't seen or spoken to them since I left. They have no hold over me."

Raphael's gaze intensified. "This isn't about the deplorable way they treated you. Though I believe I shamed them enough to force a retreat from our society over the past decade."

"That wasn't necessary."

"I disagree." He took a deep breath. "I wish it could've been more and sooner. I wish you would've told someone before you started with the Suits. I wish you would've consented to having the story told before the Elders so they could've tossed those bastards into the pit. I wish I would've seen the signs. Taken away their positions of power so they couldn't so easily cover up what they were doing."

Simon's lungs seized with the leader's words. He'd refused it all. He'd wanted to get out and forget. He moved closer to Raph's desk, not wanting to see the look in Tryst's eyes. "What are you asking me to do?"

"Rumors have reached my ears a few times over the past five years, things your parents said in passing, but it wasn't until the suicide bombing, Benson's soldiers infiltrating, that I put two and two together." He leaned forward. "I think your parents were the ones who sold Pantera to Benson."

"What?" His entire body flooded with disgust.

"Too many of our kind were taken and used as blood donors, sperm donors, even sex slaves. I asked myself, how was the enemy getting so many? It never occurred to me that two sick and twisted Pantera who believed their own cub was a—"

"Freak of nature?" Simon supplied.

"Special," Raphael countered. "Singular, and brilliant as hell. Who would've thought they'd want to punish their species in such a horrifying way?"

"You really think they've done this?"

The leader nodded. "The intel I'm getting is very strong, very compelling. They've gotten lazy in the past few years about keeping their anger at the Pantera to themselves."

His brain started to get fuzzy. "Anyone could interrogate them, Raphael..."

"I need their admission. I need to know how they did it— if they're still doing it. Who else might be involved. Who their contacts were." His brow lifted. "They trust you."

Simon laughed bitterly, his gut clenching with sickness. "They're ashamed of me. Disgusted by me."

"Maybe so," Raphael admitted. "But you're family. We have their house wired for sound. Whatever you can get from them, it'll be recorded. I just need you to try."

Shaking his head, Simon ground out, "Do you have any idea what you're asking?"

"I think so."

"I'll have to pretend I don't want to rip them apart."

"Just like you did every day of your cubhood, right? Like every time they beat you because you couldn't change, humiliated you, kept you locked in that small cage in the back bedroom of your house in hopes that it would force the cat out of you?"

A gasp rang out behind him, and Simon knew it was Tryst. So what? She knew the truth now. She'd either pity him or be disgusted by him. Neither one could breach his soul now. He was good and fully wrecked.

"If I do this," Simon told the leader of the Pantera, "get the answers you want, you'll never contact me again. You'll forget I exist."

Gold eyes flecked with jade regarded him. "Is that really what you want?"

Simon clipped him a nod.

"All right. But let me add that if you do this, brother, I'll make sure to put those assholes away for the rest of their lives, so they never hurt another Pantera. I won't need your statement of their guilt this time." His gaze softened. "And with them gone, maybe you'll finally see the Wildlands as your home once again."

Simon shook his head, laughed softly. *Impossible.* And yet, the Suit's words filled him with something he barely recognized. Something he refused to look at. Something that felt a lot like hope.

"Give me two hours," he said, turning to go. "They'll either spill their guts or slam the door in my face."

Tryst stood right in his path, her expression one he recognized. One he'd spent many years desperate to get away from.

Pity.

"Simon," she began.

The look he shot her way nearly stopped her from breathing. "Don't follow me, female. In fact, forget you ever met me. Because as soon as this is over, I'll be doing the same to you."

Chapter Nine

Her cat refused to come to her. Take her over. But did that stop her from stalking her prey?

Hell no, it did not.

Because her prey happened to also be her mate. Whether he wanted to believe it or not.

Pacing back and forth near a stand of cypress, Tryst eyed the small cottage. This was where her male had grown up. And, according to Raphael, been abused, humiliated and discarded because of something he couldn't help.

The cat inside her gave a low growl.

There you are. It's about time.

Calling the beast forth, she waited for her shift. But nothing happened. Irritation flickered through her.

"Damn you," she muttered to the beast, then took off toward the house.

Simon was already inside. She'd watched him. The two assholes who'd brought him into the world, then broken him, hadn't been all that keen on letting him in. In fact, the male had told him to go and never come back. But Simon had pushed past him and entered anyway.

He was stubborn, that was for sure. And got what he wanted, did what he wanted. Like her.

Moving quickly, quietly, stealing moves from her cat, she rounded the side of the house. As soon as she did, she heard voices coming from inside. Searching for an open window, she found one near the back. Granted, everything was being taped, but she wanted to hear—wanted to be there for him, even when he didn't want her to be.

"With the bombing, Raphael called me home," she heard Simon saying, his deep voice carrying through the window and into her ears and her heart.

She inched forward.

"Why would the leader of the Pantera call something like you back here? What help could you possibly offer? You're as worthless as a human."

Dick.

"Elijah," came a female's voice. "Save your breath. You know the cub. Lies were all that came out of his mouth before. I can't imagine it's any different now."

"That's right, Elijah," Simon agreed, his tone colder than she'd ever heard it. "All that came from me were lies. Just like now, when I'm here to save your sorry asses from the Elders' wrath."

A quick silence followed, then, "What are you talking about, mutant?"

"They know," Simon said plainly, emotionless.

Tryst climbed up onto a couple of bricks so she could see inside. The house was spotless, but smelled strange, like ancient food. Two older Pantera she'd seen maybe a handful times in town were seated near a round dining table. And then there was Simon, standing a few feet away. He was the very picture of strength and intelligence and beauty and brawn.

Her male.

Everything within her, including her cat, knew it to be true. And she wanted to sink her fangs and claws into the necks of both of these sick pieces of shit for what they'd done to him.

"Raphael and Parish know what you've been up to," Simon continued, his brow lifted. When they didn't respond, he pushed harder. "Selling Pantera to the highest bidder." He shook his head. "What were you thinking?"

The older male spoke first. "No idea what you're talking about, mutant."

Oh, shit. Was he going to pretend he knew nothing on the subject? Was bringing Simon here, hurting him, betraying him, for nothing?

"You're a fool for coming here," the male continued.

"You're right," Simon agreed calmly. "I am a fool. I had a shred of family loyalty left in me and thought I could get you both out of the

Wildlands before you're tossed to the Elders. Forget it."

He started past them, but the female darted out and grabbed his wrist. "No," she said. "Wait."

He looked down at her hand. "Wow, you're actually touching your freak cub. Make sure to wash your hands afterward." He yanked free and started for the door.

"Don't go," she called after him. "Please help us. What we did was a mistake. We were angry. We've paid a high price, seeing those disgusting Rats living here. Those half breed—"

"Mutants?" Simon finished for her.

"Female, are you insane?" the older male scolded. "He can't do anything for us. He's worthless and weak. He's the battered worm one dangles off the dock to catch the big fish."

His words, his voice, it was like hearing evil aloud. And Simon had lived through a lifetime of that. Unending torture. Too ashamed to tell... Too afraid to have them punished. No wonder he left at such a young age... Her heart sank. And she'd brought him back.

"Our idiot leader can barely stop humans from crossing our borders," the male continued. "He'll never be able to prove we sold Pantera. There's no money trail because that wasn't the payback we wanted." He dismissed Simon with a hand. "Go, mutant. We don't need the help of a damaged, good-for-nothing halfling. After all, you're the reason we did it to begin with." He stood, moved toward Simon, his face a mask of hatred and disgust. "Having to look on you every day, the shame we both felt. You were our greatest mistake."

Shaking with rage, Tryst was incapable of stopping it. Without her calling it forward, her puma emerged. And with a snarl of abject hatred and hunger, it leapt through the window and onto Simon's father.

* * * *

"Thank you, Simon," Raphael said. "You've done us a great service."

Outside the makeshift office of the leader of the Pantera, Simon finished up the business of the day. The business he never wanted to engage in again. But business that hadn't been as deeply painful as he'd believed it would be.

The terrible words and deeds of Elijah and Marie, his sperm and egg donors, weren't able to penetrate his skin anymore. As he'd stood before them, listened to their tired insults and studied their faces, which were heavily lined now from years of sour, intolerable, angry expressions, he didn't feel small and worthless and scared. Instead, he felt true pity. Their life had been nothing but regrets and hatred, and they were about to pay the ultimate price with their freedom.

Raphael walked with him as they headed out of the center of town. "I will, of course, honor our agreement, but," the Suit said, reaching out and placing a hand on Simon's shoulder, "I hope you'll return. If not to live, then at least to visit." He squeezed once before he released him. "You have friends here. And family, whether you want to believe it or not. Sometimes family has nothing to do with blood."

"I appreciate that," Simon said. And oddly, he meant it. Something had happened to him today. Something he'd never thought possible. He'd healed. Just a bit. But that bit was enough for him to recognize a few things. Seeing his parents through the eyes of a grown Pantera, one who lived a successful life of his own making, was so powerful. They looked so tiny and frail and sad. And, for the first time in forever, he felt as though he was free of them.

"Have you heard from Tryst?" Raphael asked as they headed toward the bayou.

"No." In fact, he hadn't seen her since Raph, Michel, Parish, and Keira had come rushing into his parents' house. She'd managed to take a bite out of Elijah's thigh—or her cat had—before Parish had pulled her off. But after that, she'd disappeared.

Truthfully, he hadn't stopped thinking about her since. Or worrying about her. She'd been watching, listening, and when the male he'd never again call "father" had spewed the most hateful of venom, she'd flown through the window like supergirl in fur and kicked ass.

"Do you want me to tell her anything?" Raphael asked as they stopped in front of the slow-moving water.

"Is she in trouble?"

Raphael laughed. "For snagging some skin off that old bastard? Fuck, no. We might give her a medal."

Simon's lips twitched. "She'd love that."

"What happened between you two? Was it really just...rutting?" The male's gold eyes flashed in the light of the coming sunset. "I know it's none of my business, but, she's a good female, Simon."

Nostrils flared, he glanced past the Suit to the water.

"Your experience growing up here was a nightmare I wish I would've known about and could've saved you from. But it wasn't her experience."

"I know that."

"But with that experience came a deep sense of loyalty to her kind. To me, as the leader of the Pantera."

"What about her loyalty to me?" Simon returned hotly, then wished he could steal the words back.

"You mean to the male she rutted?" A grin touched the male's mouth. "Or to her mate?"

Simon dragged a hand through his hair.

"Would you wish her to find another?" the Suit asked.

Nostrils flared, a low growl rumbled in Simon's chest. Just the thought—

"Because if you really don't want her, if you truly can't forgive her for following through on the command of her leader, you need to tell her. Release her and let her have a life with someone who will love and commit to her."

Where an hour ago, he'd felt nothing but pity as his parents called him "mutant" and "a mistake," now he felt staggering pain and rage—at just the idea of releasing Tryst, giving her to another male. It was true. He had no cat. He was certain of that. But something clawed and scratched at his insides at the thought of Tryst in another male's arms.

Before he could say anything to Raph, the soft but unmistakable sound of paws hitting earth rent the air. Both males turned to see a massive black puma entering the clearing. When it got about six feet away, it stopped and sat back on its haunches.

Waiting.

"I'll leave you here," Raphael said. "My mate and daughter made dinner tonight. Can't be late."

Simon nodded, but his eyes remained on the puma. "Good-bye, Raph."

"No," the leader of the Pantera said as he walked away. "I'll see you later, Simon."

Chapter Ten

Mine.

This male.

The taste of blood still on her tongue, the cat pushed from its sitting position and advanced. It was true he carried no shifting puma within him, but it was there—in a different way. In his heart and mind, and in the blood running through his veins. In some ways, it had made him even more powerful than the rest of the Pantera.

He didn't need to shift to be a formidable warrior.

The ones who had made him couldn't understand such beauty. They saw his difference as wrong. She and her female form, Tryst, saw him as special.

Mine.

As if he heard her thoughts, he came toward her, stopping when she did. Dark blue eyes to her pale blue, she stared up at him. After a moment, he exhaled heavily, reaching for her. She felt his hand on her massive neck, and instantly she began to purr.

"I'll never be this, Tryst," he said in an even voice.

The cat had no choice but to retreat, and in seconds Tryst stood before him. Naked. Completely at ease with herself. "You're more."

He stared at her, his eyes clinging to her eyes despite her obvious nudity.

"You may not be able to call a cat forward," she said. "But you brought a female out of hers, out of the self-imposed prison she'd been hiding inside of. You showed her what it was like to be touched, to feel, to be vulnerable and happy."

He reached out and brushed his fingers over her cheek. "I don't know if I belong here, Tryst. Don't know if I can be happy here."

"You don't have to live here. I'd be content in my female form forever if it was with you."

His eyes drew sadness and he shook his head. "I would never do that to you."

Didn't he understand? "But you'd have me live without you? I'm your mate, Simon."

"Why do you believe that?" Even with the question on his lips, a growl vibrated in his throat.

She covered his hand with her own and smiled softly. "Tell me you don't. Tell me you don't and I'll walk away right now. I'll let you leave and I won't chase you." Tears pricked her eyes and she cursed inwardly. The hardass Hunter who handled pain like it was nothing at all was breaking at the thought of this male walking out of her life.

"Listen to me," she continued. "I know you're scared to trust me again. I don't blame you. Especially after what you've been through. But I'm so sorry I betrayed you."

His jaw tightened. "You had a duty to Raphael and the Pantera."

"I wish that was the full reason," she said, her heart squeezing with worry.

His brows drew together. "It wasn't?"

She shook her head. "I wanted you to come back here. For me, and for you. I'd heard you say things in your sleep about not having a cat inside you and how you were a worthless cub..."

He dropped his hand and snarled, shame glistening in his eyes.

"I see what you're doing," she said, her hands going to his face now, forcing him to look at her, deep into her eyes. "Don't go there with me. Not ever. I'm not them. I see you, Simon. Do you understand me? I see you."

"I know you do," he said on a rush of breath.

Again, her heart squeezed. "Really?"

His eyes locked with hers. They were stormy blue, but it was a storm that raged from love.

"I wanted to bring you here," she continued, her voice breaking with emotion, "because I was hoping you'd change your feelings about the Wildlands. I was hoping that if you had a cat, it could be released by someone who cared about you so deeply you actually felt it, knew it in your heart—without them around, without those horrible pieces of—"

She started to cry, for real now. Great big tears forming in her eyes and falling on her cheeks. "Goddess, I'm a mess. This isn't how I am. Or wasn't. It's tearing me up, Simon. I didn't know I could feel like this."

"I understand. I do. Hush now." He took her in his arms and held her close. "Love does some crazy shit, *ma chère*."

She let him hold her. For several seconds. Reveled in his warmth and protection. But it couldn't be forever. Not until she said what she needed to say. Pulling away, her eyes found his once again. "Listen—"

"Kitten, you don't have to say anything more."

"Yes, I do," she insisted, passionately. "If you can't be mine…" Her voice broke again. "If you can't…will you at least forgive me before you release me?"

He gazed at her, his eyes filled with something she couldn't name. And then he leaned in and kissed the top of her head, whispered into her hair, "I can't, Tryst."

"Oh, Simon…" she cried, wanting to die, wanting to run, wanting to scream and beg and—

"I can't release you."

Tryst froze, pulled back. "What?"

He tipped her chin up and wiped the tears from her eyes. Then he kissed her gently on the mouth. "Oh, kitten, there's nothing to forgive. It was a miracle. I actually found peace here. For the first time in my life." He smiled at her, lovingly, adoringly. "And I found you. My mate."

Her heart filled to bursting and she smiled through a fresh batch of tears. "Yes. Yours. Out of the Wildlands—"

"And in," he finished.

Crying out, she threw her arms around his neck and kissed him, hard and long and sweet and true. And when he eased back, his nose resting against hers, and whispered the words, "My home" and "My Tryst" against her lips, she finally understood the true meaning of the word "*mate*."

It wasn't about claiming at all. It was about connecting.

Two Hearts.

Two minds.

One soul.

Forever.

* * * *

Also from 1001 Dark Nights and Alexandra Ivy and Laura Wright, discover Rage/Killian.

Sign up for the 1001 Dark Nights Newsletter
and be entered to win a Tiffany Key necklace.

There's a contest every month!

Go to www.1001DarkNights.com to subscribe!

As a bonus, all subscribers will receive a free
1001 Dark Nights story
The First Night
by Lexi Blake & M.J. Rose

Turn the page for a full list of the
1001 Dark Nights fabulous novellas...

Discover 1001 Dark Nights Collection Three

HIDDEN INK by Carrie Ann Ryan
A Montgomery Ink Novella

BLOOD ON THE BAYOU by Heather Graham
A Cafferty & Quinn Novella

SEARCHING FOR MINE by Jennifer Probst
A Searching For Novella

DANCE OF DESIRE by Christopher Rice

ROUGH RHYTHM by Tessa Bailey
A Made In Jersey Novella

DEVOTED by Lexi Blake
A Masters and Mercenaries Novella

Z by Larissa Ione
A Demonica Underworld Novella

FALLING UNDER YOU by Laurelin Paige
A Fixed Trilogy Novella

EASY FOR KEEPS by Kristen Proby
A Boudreaux Novella

UNCHAINED by Elisabeth Naughton
An Eternal Guardians Novella

HARD TO SERVE by Laura Kaye
A Hard Ink Novella

DRAGON FEVER by Donna Grant
A Dark Kings Novella

KAYDEN/SIMON by Alexandra Ivy/Laura Wright
A Bayou Heat Novella

STRUNG UP by Lorelei James
A Blacktop Cowboys® Novella

MIDNIGHT UNTAMED by Lara Adrian
A Midnight Breed Novella

TRICKED by Rebecca Zanetti
A Dark Protectors Novella

DIRTY WICKED by Shayla Black
A Wicked Lovers Novella

A SEDUCTIVE INVITATION by Lauren Blakely
A Seductive Nights New York Novella

SWEET SURRENDER by Liliana Hart
A MacKenzie Family Novella

Visit www.1001DarkNights.com for more information.

Discover 1001 Dark Nights Collection One

FOREVER WICKED by Shayla Black
CRIMSON TWILIGHT by Heather Graham
CAPTURED IN SURRENDER by Liliana Hart
SILENT BITE: A SCANGUARDS WEDDING by Tina Folsom
DUNGEON GAMES by Lexi Blake
AZAGOTH by Larissa Ione
NEED YOU NOW by Lisa Renee Jones
SHOW ME, BABY by Cherise Sinclair
ROPED IN by Lorelei James
TEMPTED BY MIDNIGHT by Lara Adrian
THE FLAME by Christopher Rice
CARESS OF DARKNESS by Julie Kenner

Also from 1001 Dark Nights

TAME ME by J. Kenner

Visit www.1001DarkNights.com for more information.

Discover 1001 Dark Nights Collection Two

WICKED WOLF by Carrie Ann Ryan
WHEN IRISH EYES ARE HAUNTING by Heather Graham
EASY WITH YOU by Kristen Proby
MASTER OF FREEDOM by Cherise Sinclair
CARESS OF PLEASURE by Julie Kenner
ADORED by Lexi Blake
HADES by Larissa Ione
RAVAGED by Elisabeth Naughton
DREAM OF YOU by Jennifer L. Armentrout
STRIPPED DOWN by Lorelei James
RAGE/KILLIAN by Alexandra Ivy/Laura Wright
DRAGON KING by Donna Grant
PURE WICKED by Shayla Black
HARD AS STEEL by Laura Kaye
STROKE OF MIDNIGHT by Lara Adrian
ALL HALLOWS EVE by Heather Graham
KISS THE FLAME by Christopher Rice
DARING HER LOVE by Melissa Foster
TEASED by Rebecca Zanetti
THE PROMISE OF SURRENDER by Liliana Hart

Also from 1001 Dark Nights

THE SURRENDER GATE By Christopher Rice
SERVICING THE TARGET By Cherise Sinclair

Visit www.1001DarkNights.com for more information.

About Alexandra Ivy and Laura Wright

Alexandra Ivy is a *New York Times* and *USA Today* bestselling author of the Guardians of Eternity, as well as the Sentinels, Dragons of Eternity and ARES series. After majoring in theatre she decided she prefers to bring her characters to life on paper rather than stage. She lives in Missouri with her family. Visit her website at alexandraivy.com.

New York Times and USA Today Bestselling Author, Laura Wright is passionate about romantic fiction. Though she has spent most of her life immersed in acting, singing and competitive ballroom dancing, when she found the world of writing and books and endless cups of coffee she knew she was home. Laura is the author of the bestselling Mark of the Vampire series and the USA Today bestselling series, Bayou Heat, which she co-authors with Alexandra Ivy.

Laura lives in Los Angeles with her husband, two young children and three loveable dogs.

Kill Without Mercy
Ares Security Book 1
By Alexandra Ivy
Now Available

From the hellhole of a Taliban prison to sweet freedom, five brave military heroes have made it home—and they're ready to take on the civilian missions no one else can. Individually they're intimidating. Together they're invincible. They're the men of ARES Security.

Rafe Vargas is only in Newton, Iowa, to clear out his late grandfather's small house. As the covert ops specialist for ARES Security, he's eager to get back to his new life in Texas. But when he crosses paths with Annie White, a haunted beauty with skeletons in her closet, he can't just walk away—not when she's clearly in danger...

There's a mysterious serial killer on the loose with a link to Annie's dark past. And the closer he gets, the deeper Rafe's instinct to protect kicks in. But even with his considerable skill, Annie's courage, and his ARES buddies behind him, the slaying won't stop. Now it's only a matter of time before Annie's next—unless they can unravel a history of deadly lies that won't be buried.

* * * *

Friday nights in Houston meant crowded bars, loud music and ice-cold beer. It was a tradition that Rafe and his friends had quickly adapted to suit their own tastes when they moved to Texas five months ago.

After all, none of them were into the dance scene. They were too old for half-naked coeds and casual hookups. And none of them wanted to have to scream over pounding music to have a decent conversation.

Instead, they'd found The Saloon, a small, cozy bar with lots of polished wood, a jazz band that played softly in the background, and a handful of locals who knew better than to bother the other customers. Oh, and the finest tequila in the city.

They even had their own table that was reserved for them every Friday night.

Tucked in a back corner, it was shrouded in shadows and well away from the long bar that ran the length of one wall. A perfect spot to observe without being observed.

And best of all, situated so no one could sneak up from behind.

It might have been almost two years since they'd returned from the war, but none of them had forgotten. Lowering your guard, even for a second, could mean death.

Lesson. Fucking. Learned.

Tonight, however, it was only Rafe and Hauk at the table, both of them sipping tequila and eating peanuts from a small bucket.

Lucas was still in Washington D.C., working his contacts to help drum up business for their new security business, ARES. Max had remained at their new offices, putting the final touches on his precious forensics lab, and Teagan was on his way to the bar after installing a computer system that would give Homeland Security a hemorrhage if they knew what he was doing.

Leaning back in his chair, Rafe intended to spend the night relaxing after a long week of hassling with the red tape and bullshit regulations that went into opening a new business, when he made the mistake of checking his messages.

"Shit."

He tossed his cellphone on the polished surface of the wooden table, a tangled ball of emotions lodged in the pit of his stomach.

Across the table Hauk sipped his tequila and studied Rafe with a lift of his brows.

At a glance, the two men couldn't be more different.

Rafe had dark hair that had grown long enough to touch the collar of his white button-down shirt along with dark eyes that were lushly framed by long, black lashes. His skin remained tanned dark bronze despite the fact it was late September, and his body was honed with muscles that came from working on the small ranch he'd just purchased, not the gym.

Hauk, on the other hand, had inherited his Scandinavian father's pale blond hair that he kept cut short, and brilliant blue eyes that held a cunning intelligence. He had a narrow face with sculpted features that were usually set in a stern expression.

And it wasn't just their outward appearance that made them so different.

Rafe was hot tempered, passionate and willing to trust his gut instincts.

Hauk was aloof, calculating, and mind-numbingly anal. Not that Hauk would admit he was OCD. He preferred to call himself detail-oriented.

Which was exactly why he was a successful sniper. Rafe, on the other hand, had been trained in combat rescue. He was capable of making quick decisions, and ready to change strategies on the fly.

"Trouble?" Hauk demanded.

Rafe grimaced. "The real estate agent left a message saying she has a buyer for my grandfather's house."

Hauk looked predictably confused. Rafe had been bitching about the need to get rid of his grandfather's house since the old man's death a year ago.

"Shouldn't that be good news?"

"It would be if I didn't have to travel to Newton to clean it out," Rafe said.

"Aren't there people you can hire to pack up the shit and send it to you?"

"Not in the middle of fucking nowhere."

Hauk's lips twisted into a humorless smile. "I've been in the middle of fucking nowhere, amigo, and it ain't Kansas," he said, the shadows from the past darkening his eyes.

"Newton's in Iowa, but I get your point," Rafe conceded. He did his best to keep the memories in the past where they belonged. Most of the time he was successful. Other times the demons refused to be leashed. "Okay, it's not the hell hole we crawled out of, but the town might as well be living in another century. I'll have to go deal with my grandfather's belongings myself."

Hauk reached to pour himself another shot of tequila from the bottle that had been waiting for them in the center of the table.

Like Rafe, he was dressed in an Oxford shirt, although his was blue instead of white, and he was wearing black dress pants instead of jeans.

"I know you think it's a pain, but it's probably for the best."

Rafe glared at his friend. The last thing he wanted was to drive a thousand miles to pack up the belongings of a cantankerous old man who'd never forgiven Rafe's father for walking away from Iowa. "Already trying to get rid of me?"

"Hell no. Of the five of us, you're the..."

"I'm afraid to ask," Rafe muttered as Hauk hesitated.

"The glue," he at last said.

Rafe gave a bark of laughter. He'd been called a lot of things over the years. Most of them unrepeatable. But glue was a new one. "What the hell does that mean?"

Hauk settled back in his seat. "Lucas is the smooth-talker, Max is the heart, Teagan is the brains and I'm the organizer." The older man shrugged. "You're the one who holds us all together. ARES would never have happened without you."

Rafe couldn't argue. After returning to the States, the five of them had been transferred to separate hospitals to treat their numerous injuries. It would have been easy to drift apart. The natural instinct was to avoid anything that could remind them of the horror they'd endured.

But Rafe had quickly discovered that returning to civilian life wasn't a simple matter of buying a home and getting a 9-to-5 job.

He couldn't bear the thought of being trapped in a small cubicle eight hours a day, or returning to an empty condo that would never be a home.

It felt way too much like the prison he'd barely escaped.

Discover More Alexandra Ivy and Laura Wright

Rage/Killian
Bayou Heat Novellas

RAGE
Rage might be an aggressive Hunter by nature, but the gorgeous male has never had a problem charming the females. All except Lucie Gaudet. Of course, the lovely Geek is a born troublemaker, and it was no surprise to Rage when she was kicked out of the Wildlands.

But now the Pantera need a first-class hacker to stop the potential destruction of their people. And it's up to Rage to convince Lucie to help. Can the two forget the past—and their sizzling attraction—to save the Pantera?

KILLIAN
Gorgeous, brutal, aggressive, and human, Killian O'Roarke wants only two things: to get rid of the Pantera DNA he's been infected with, and get back to the field. But the decorated Army Ranger never bargained on meeting the woman—the female—of his dreams on his mission to the Wildlands.

Rosalie lost her mate to a human, and now the Hunter despises them all. In fact, she thinks they're good for only one thing: barbeque. But this one she's guarding is testing her beliefs. He is proud and kind, and also knows the pain of loss. But in a time of war between their species, isn't any chance of love destined for destruction?

On behalf of 1001 Dark Nights,
Liz Berry and M.J. Rose would like to thank ~

Steve Berry
Doug Scofield
Kim Guidroz
Jillian Stein
InkSlinger PR
Dan Slater
Asha Hossain
Chris Graham
Pamela Jamison
Jessica Johns
Dylan Stockton
Richard Blake
BookTrib After Dark
The Dinner Party Show
and Simon Lipskar

Made in the USA
Middletown, DE
10 August 2017